The Good Life Elsewhere

VLADIMIR LORCHENKOV

TRANSLATED BY ROSS UFBERG

ИНСТИТУТ ПЕРЕВОДА

Published with the support of the Institute of Literary Translation, Russia

THE GOOD LIFE ELSEWHERE

 New Vessel Press

www.newvesselpress.com

First published in Russian in 2008 as *Vse tam budem*

Copyright © 2008 Vladimir Lorchenkov
Translation Copyright © 2014 New Vessel Press

Library of Congress Cataloging-in-Publication Data
Lorchenkov, Vladimir
[Vse tam budem. English]
The Good Life Elsewhere / by Vladimir Lorchenko; translation by Ross Ufberg.
p. cm.
ISBN 978-1-939931-01-6
Library of Congress Control Number 2013938584
I. Moldova—Fiction.

We're all a little Assyrian.
Capt. John Yossarian

... and a bit Moldovan, too.
Serafim Botezatu

1

"Here you are! Italy, our Italy."

Serafim Botezatu narrowed his eyes and blinked, but the city spreading out beneath him in the valleys between the hills didn't disappear. Buildings of white stone were just as blinding as the joy Serafim and his forty-five fellow travelers—Moldovans all—were feeling. They were standing in a little grove on a hill beside the capital of capitals, Rome herself, and none of them could believe what was happening. Finally, they'd made it to Italy. Finally, life had become clear and simple. Just like it used to be, like it was in their childhoods. They'd left behind Larga, their village in Moldova. They'd left behind the poverty, the Moldovan devastation, the repellent earth that, no matter which way you worked it, when you planted corn you reaped just the husks. In front of them was Rome. Which meant, in front of them was breezy construction work, or some other menial labor. In comparison to toiling on the land, what wasn't a breeze? And for the women, there was work cleaning house for wealthy Italians – to whom, with a bit of luck, they might even end up getting hitched.

Serafim looked around at his fellow travelers. He was nearly guilty of the sin of pride. After all, it was thanks to him they'd been able to extract themselves from the swamp at the end of a small and dirty river, where they'd been dumped by the runners who'd smuggled them into Italy.

"That's it. We go no further. It's too dangerous," said the driver, a dark-haired youth with a painful resemblance to a gypsy, which didn't sit well with the Largans.

"But if you throw in an extra ten euros a nose, I'll take you to the doorstep of the Roman buildings."

The Largans refused. Over the course of the four days they'd been en route, the driver had taken an extra sixty euros from each of them, on top of the four thousand euros they'd all paid for the trip and the promise of a job upon arrival. There was ten for lodging, twenty each for grub, and thirty euros to bribe the Slovak policeman.

"We'll go the rest of the road ourselves," the group decided, especially since they had Serafim. Everyone in Larga knew that Serafim Botezatu had had a painful love affair with Italy for a long time. As a ten-year-old boy he'd found a photo book called *Views of Rome* in the half-ruined library, and since then he was lost to the world. He'd tracked down a textbook somewhere in the regional center to teach himself Italian and read everything in any way connected with Italy, the country of his dreams. Back then, in the eighties, this wasn't smiled upon. But did anybody know in those days that in twenty years' time, tens of thousands of Moldovans would make their way to Italy to work? And that Serafim, whom everybody had laughed at—from the village shepherds and their helpers to the chairman of the collective farm—would become an authority in Larga?

Serafim labored over Italian for twenty years, made do with bread and water and waited and waited for fate to deliver him to Rome. And here he was, a stone's throw away from the city of his dreams: all atremble, he was even a bit sad it was happening so quickly.

"Twenty years," mumbled Serafim wistfully. "Twenty whole years …"

The villagers waited respectfully. The only one who

The Good Life Elsewhere

knew Italian, and the one they hung all their hopes on, was Serafim. Him, and him alone.

He was listening to the lapping of the water.

"This – is a river. Rome's not far away. In Rome there's only one river, and it's called the Tiber. It stands to reason, we're standing on the banks of the Tiber!" he declared.

The people silently followed his conclusions, amazed at the broad span of his mind. Serafim, recalling with perfect lucidity how Rome looked in pictures in *Echo of the Planet*, a magazine he'd subscribed to back when there still was such a thing as USSR-wide subscriptions, led the people farther from the water, into a grove. They were waiting for the morning. Meanwhile, the sun hadn't yet lifted its veil from Rome to show them the city, that sleeping beauty, in her full glory. Rapture shone on all their faces, but their reasons were different. Serafim, for example, was already savoring his visits to the museums and theaters, and his sublime walks through the crooked streets of Rome. The others looked at Rome from a strictly practical point of view, as a place where Lady Luck would finally flash them a smile. They'd find work. Of course, Serafim would have to work, too: he needed to pay back the four thousand euros he'd gone to such great pains to collect. But that was of secondary concern … One way or another, they all had the same goal: Rome!

"Take a look at the city," said Serafim anxiously. "This city was built upon hills. A majestic picture! True, I don't see the Coliseum, and Saint Peter's Basilica hasn't come into view yet, but the city is so great that, after all, you can't see everything at once!"

The citizens of Larga, a village two miles long and only slightly more than that across, inhaled with delight.

"Serafim," Rodika Kretsu, one of the group, spoke up timidly, "when can we start down for the city? I'm dying to take a bath, change my clothes and have a nap. On a bed, not the damp ground."

The people began to whisper approvingly, like autumn leaves in a grove. For four whole days the bus carrying the villagers had traveled only at night, though they bore official documents listing them as two curling teams and two underwater swim teams. By day, the driver pulled off into the bushes at the side of the road and camouflaged the vehicle with shrubbery. He especially forbade the villagers from making noise or stepping out of the bus. For four days, as Serafim colorfully put it, they'd lived through another Turkish Yoke when Moldovans suffered terribly under Ottoman rule. Many of them even complained they'd shrunk in size. But the driver was intractable and strict.

"Whoever doesn't want to go to Italy can clear right out of this bus," he shouted at the unhappy cargo.

Everybody wanted to go to Italy, so for four days they waited patiently. And to remain in place now, when they were just a half a mile from their sacred goal, was something they didn't have the strength for. Serafim understood them; he didn't have the strength, either. The entire insufferable bus ride, he hadn't had the chance to see a single Italian city by daylight. Everything was done at night. Once in a while, a cop would pull the bus over and Serafim, hidden inside a blanket and with a sinking heart, peered through a small window and watched the driver negotiate for the right to keep going. Then the driver would come running into the back of the bus, announce in a sinister whisper the amount of the bribe each of them would have to pay, take the money and bound back onto the road like a bat out of hell. Nobody was sorry about the money. They would've gladly paid in blood. For the villagers, once they reached Italy, their past sins would be redeemed and they'd gain possession of a new life. What difference did it make how much money they left behind in the past, when there were fat paychecks of seven hundred, nine hundred euros a month in the future? If somebody had told them to commit suicide and Italy would be waiting for them in the afterlife, they would have done it. In this respect, noticed the erudite Serafim, they were like the residents of Europe awaiting the Apocalypse in the year 1000.

"People were ready for anything," Serafim whispered with sorrow. "They turned into wild animals, lost all hope …"

But he understood: it wasn't the Largans' fault. Everyone had grown painfully weary of life in Moldova today. But Moldovans have never been a people capable of revolt. There was only one option left: to run. When representatives of a tourism agency showed up in Larga, everybody got excited. The firm, it was rumored, sent people to Italy. Father Paisii, the fine-looking priest who served two competing confessions—the Metropolitan Church of Moldova and the Metropolitan Church of Bessarabia——read a prayer of gratitude for the occasion in the ramshackle village church. He was even planning on a Cross Procession, but the weather hadn't allowed for it. A cold hail cut down the remnants of the late harvest, and, turning gradually into freezing rain, made the roads soupier than purée.

"We'll make do without the Procession, Father," enjoined the representatives of the tourism agency. After suffering through a prayer in their honor, they began the meeting in the village clubhouse.

"Who wants to work in Italy?"

523 people lived in Larga. 1045 hands went up in the air. Every adult present, in an effort to get noticed, put up both hands. The odd number was on account of the one-armed war veteran, the watchman Sergei Mokanu.

"We've no strength left!" said Postolaki, the former chairman, putting his hand over his heart. "We plow like the devil. From morning to night we crawl like worms and we still don't have two coins to rub together. A year goes by, we don't see any money. Well, that's not true. Yesterday I saw fifty thousand lei – on the TV show *Lotto-Bingo*. But nothing in real life. We're sick and tired of this place. How do we get out? What do we have to do? Show us what's what!"

The wheeler-dealers chuckled good-naturedly, clasped their hands together and began to show the villagers what was what. First of all, they explained, a trip to Italy is not one of life's cheaper pleasures. It would cost four thousand euros …

After the town medical attendant served valerian tea to calm the nerves of the seven people who fell ill following the announcement of the sum, the slave traders continued. According to them, not everybody could leave at once. Three thousand people from all across Moldova were already signed up, and that would be a crowd. They suggested transporting the villagers in small groups, as they came up with the means. Where to find those means was up to the villagers. They could take out loans or sell their land. It was every man for himself, however he could manage it.

"But if I were in your shoes," said the man in the suit, "I wouldn't be afraid and I wouldn't be sorry. What the hell do you need Moldova for, if you're already practically in Italy?"

"And what if things start improving *here* as soon as we get *there*?" came a voice from the audience.

"Well, what if?" countered the wheeler-dealer. "Stay in Moldova and wait for the European Union – Moldova Cooperation Plan to be implemented. Wait for the tenfold increase in the living standard your president's been talking about for six years now …"

After the villagers had a laugh and gave the speaker an

ovation, he concluded his speech. They weren't going to let Moldovans into the West just like that. They'd have to travel disguised as sports team. For a start, the first group of forty or fifty people would be divided into four teams. Two curling teams and two underwater swim teams. Nobody was really going to have to swim or stand around on the ice, of course. The main thing was to get the proper papers.

And the papers materialized. Forty-five underwater swimmers and curlers from the village of Larga, plus Serafim Botezatu, who'd been dreaming of Italy his entire life, were about to see their dreams come true.

Serafim felt like a worm who's just found an apple. The sun rose higher over Rome, once again blinding Serafim's rejoicing soul. He began quietly descending the hill without bothering to look around. He was sure the entire group was following. In his mind, Serafim carefully repeated the phrase he was going to say to the first Italian who crossed his path. After that, he'd ask for directions to a church. He knew that in Italian churches, they often fed the Moldovans and gave them work. He reached the bottom of the hill and turned onto a paved road. It wasn't of the best quality, of course, but really, isn't that always the case in industrial areas? In front of him loomed the spine of a workman who, apparently deciding not to wait for a bus, had started walking.

"*Buongiorno*," muttered Serafim, in relatively passable Italian. "Respected Citizen of Italy, descendant of the Roman Caesars and the courageous Bersaglieri, *buongiorno*! I am glad to greet you on behalf of the fraternal Moldovan people. Would you mind telling me where the nearest church is, and please, don't inform the police on us! I offer you my gratitude! A million compliments!"

Serafim could physically feel the respect of his fellow villagers behind him. The workman looked around and picked up his step. "I've scared him, I'm sure," thought Serafim. He understood how the situation might look dubious: a lone Roman, being pursued by a throng of dirty-chinned, stinking, wrinkled Moldovans. A scary sight! Serafim started running and caught up with the Italian. He grabbed him by the arm and shouted:

"Respected Citizen of Italy, descendant of the Roman Caesars and the courageous Bersaglieri, *buongiorno*! Don't be frightened! I am glad to greet you on behalf of the fraternal Moldovan people!"

The terrified Roman glanced at the Moldovans gathered around him and silently tried to tear himself away. Serafim smiled as wide as he could and attempted to explain one more time.

"Listen, heir of the Roman Caesars and the courageous Bersaglieri. I am a representative of the fraternal Moldovan people. We've come to you, to Italy, to perform the crummy jobs you Italians don't want. We're not your enemies. I am glad to greet you. Tell me, where's the church here?"

The Italian took his hand back with a frown and wiped it off. Slowly his eyes became clear, intelligent. He tried explaining something to them with gestures.

"What's going on, Serafim?" asked Chairman Postolaki, smiling widely so as not to the scare the Italian. "What, your Italian's no good?"

"It should be alright," said Serafim, guiltily acquitting himself. "But I can't make any guarantees. Practice makes perfect, but I've had nobody to speak it with."

"Oh, don't start with your 'perfect' business," said Postolaki threateningly. Even when angry, he couldn't let a chance slip by to make a pun: "Practice didn't even make you *im*perfect!"

The foreigner, who'd been observing the squabble with a surprised look on his face, spoke up.

"What, you're Moldovans? You should have just said so. What are you messing with my head for? What is this, *Candid Camera?*"

"So you're from Moldova, too?" said Postolaki, overjoyed. "It's great to meet a countryman!"

"Yeah," said the countryman, exhibiting no signs of joy. "It's not such a rarity in these parts ..."

"Well," said Postolaki, putting his hand on the other fellow's shoulder. "Show us around! Where's the closest church?"

"What for?" asked the man, dumbfounded.

"What do you mean, *What for?* Work and food. Listen, don't you worry," said Postolaki, understanding his countryman in his own way, "we're not looking to crowd anybody out. Come on, come on."

The man didn't understand a thing. He followed behind Postolaki, who, for his part, waved his arms and inhaled a lungful of air, happy everything had worked out so well.

"Here you are! Italy, our Italy," he said. "By the way, brother, where's the famous Coliseum you folks have here?"

The countryman, pulling himself away rudely from Postolaki's embrace, took off down a side street. "Lunatics!" he shouted.

The chairman was about to lament the fact that Moldovans are so inconsiderate and mean to each other, when he saw Serafim slowly slinking down a wall on the side of a building. Serafim slid down onto the pavement, unable to pull his eyes away from something in the sky. Postolaki followed his glance, already knowing ...

While Postolaki had been attempting to enter into a conversation with the Moldovan they'd encountered, Serafim had tried to figure out what was wrong with his Italian language skills. He'd learned everything from the textbook, hadn't he? True, Serafim recalled as if it were yesterday, there had been no title page on the book he'd been given at the regional library. There was no *official* way Serafim could be sure he'd learned Italian and not, say, Chinese. That was a risk he'd knowingly undertaken. On the other hand ... Could he really have spent his whole life in vain?

Serafim felt a mass of questions bubbling up inside him. He stood up, almost rocking in the wind, but there was nobody he could ask these questions to. Usually, you seek advice from people you know. But Serafim didn't know a soul in this city. He wasn't even—and his heart froze when he realized this—he wasn't even sure what city he was in. He hadn't seen signs saying "Rome" anywhere. No – all this doubting was complete nonsense, a delusion! Nonetheless, Serafim lifted his head and noticed a banner in the gap between two beautiful clouds.

One. Two. Boom. Boom. Serafim threw back his head and began to lose consciousness. Before he did, he was able to catch the surprised look on the face of Chairman Postolaki. And even before that, he had time to see – precisely to see, and not to read – what was written, what was written on the banner:

"WELCOME TO CHISINAU!!"

2

MARIA WAS PLANNING ON HANGING HERSELF FROM THE acacia tree in the yard. Her husband, Vasily Lungu, could give a damn. He was extremely angry with Maria for the four thousand euros she'd paid for the voyage to Rome and a job in Italy. His wife's guilt was not assuaged by the fact that she'd been swindled.

"It could happen to anyone," frowned Vasily at the village drinking sessions, turning around the muddy sediments of the wine in his mouth. "You all were taken in by those swindlers. They led you through Moldova by night. They let you off outside of Chisinau. I agree – I can't blame Maria for that. But who, if not her, infected us with that idiotic, childish dream about Italy?"

Thanks to that dream, Vasily had sold his tractor (though it *was* old), and gone into debt for one and a half thousand euros. The couple calculated that Maria would send home three hundred euros a month from Italy and, at that rate, they'd have the tractor and their farm back in a year.

"The tractor's nonnegotiable." Vasily shook his finger at his wife. "No tractor – nothing doing."

Maria breathed a bitter sigh. She knew about Vasily's extraordinary attachment to the tractor. It started in 1978, when Lungu, a peasant, was sent to attend a course for mechanics. Having discovered the world and machinery, as Vasily himself put it, he returned to the village with a tractor and a huge sense of self-importance. Alas, when Moldova gained its independence and lost its last remaining bits of prosperity, the need for Vasily's tractor fell off. The villagers had no money for diesel anyhow, and they worked the land as in the days of old. With their hands. But Lungu, notwithstanding his wife's exhortations, wouldn't give up or sell his iron horse. It wasn't until that very day in 2001 that Maria, tormented by poverty and wanting to escape, convinced him to temporarily sell his tractor.

"And then we'll buy it back!" she promised grandly. "Trust me."

Unfortunately, the forty-four underwater swimmers and curlers from Larga fell into the hands of crooks. Crooks who led the people through Moldova for four whole days, dumped them out onto the marshy ground near the Byk River—the very river that the local genius Serafim Botezatu took for the Tiber—and disappeared, just like that. When he found out he wasn't getting his tractor back, Vasily fell into despair. When Maria returned home, first he beat her, then he stopped talking to his wife at all. Maria realized she'd never make it to Italy. She couldn't imagine where she'd ever get the money for it, and so she decided to hang herself. True, she was helped along toward that decision.

"Either way," Vasily decided, "I'll never forgive you. And I'll thrash you till the end of your days, woman, like an ugly old dog. But God forbid I snuff the life out of you with my own hands. It'd be a sin. It's better if you'd just snuff it out yourself."

And in the course of a single day, these words grew inside Maria like a bean sprout beneath the red sun in rich, black springtime soil.

"I'm off to hang myself, Vasily," she said to her husband, holding back tears. "Our life is darkness. I'm tired."

"Don't even think about climbing up the walnut tree," he said, without glancing up from his pocket Bible. "Or

I'll take you down off there and beat you to death. You're going to break off the lower branches, and that's where the nuts grow biggest."

"Then I'll hang myself from the acacia," Maria offered. "The branches are stronger."

"Well, now, that's another story," said Vasily, and bit his lip. "Hang yourself from the acacia. And stay until the Second Coming."

Maria, knowing her husband's kind heart, went to the acacia, tightened the rope and stood on a stool beneath the noose. Nobody emerged from the house. "He's hiding behind the door," she thought to herself. And she noticed people staring at her from neighboring windows. "They'll pull me down straight away," said the woman, and she jumped. First, it was her own jump that made her swing. Then, it was the wind.

Maria swung on the acacia all through the following week.

3

Vasily Lungu turned out to be the only resident of Larga who *didn't* dream of making it to Italy.

"It doesn't exist, this Italy you keep talking about!" he would yell during village drinking bouts. "Has anyone ever seen it? Huh? That's right!"

The only one who could challenge Lungu was Father Paisii, Larga's priest. Everyone knew for a fact that his wife Elizaveta, the parish *Matushka*, had gone to Italy in 1999, using the money her ministering husband earned performing last rites, christenings, and requiem services. And since the land near Larga was barren and the peasants were poor, everybody knew the priest never swallowed a piece of bread he didn't pay for. And he always paid full price.

"All day long, like a cursed man, I pray for rain, I offer benedictions, and all for a sack of beans," Paisii would complain bitterly to his wife when she called from Bologna, where she'd found work as a housemaid. "I barely earn enough to feed myself and the kids. At least, if you could send some money ..."

For a while, Elizaveta, the priest's wife, did send three hundred euros a month to her husband and three kids. Then she stopped. A year later she sent five hundred euros. Then silence for a year. Father Paisii wore himself out, tried everything, was even planning on appealing to the Red Cross or some other sort of Organization for the Search for Missing Priests' Wives of Larga when Matushka Elizaveta turned up. Oh, did she turn up.

"Darling," she said into the receiver, puffing away at a cigarette, "I've decided to stay here and link my fate with Adriano. Don't be jealous. He's a real man, a Man with a capital M. I'm sorry, I won't be coming back to Larga, or Moldova. To that dump? After being in Italy? By the way, I've become a completely liberated woman. And I've found a job. Actually, Adriano found me a job. Where?"

It turned out, the woman once known as Matushka Elizaveta had become the secretary at the Center for Modern Art and Atheism. After breaking the news to her husband, she hung up the phone. Father Paisii cried the whole night through, and by morning he'd managed to fall asleep. He dreamed of Elizaveta in a miniskirt. She licked her lips and gave Paisii a wink. Twirling a cigarette in her hands, she said, "Got a light?" When Paisii shrugged his shoulders, Elizaveta disappeared. She said a reproachful goodbye: "You don't have a light, but I'm one hot broad, see. You better stay in Larga, you knucklehead!"

Paisii woke up broken and convinced that, in the end, Italy *did* in fact exist. After all, that accursed bitch, that cheap prostitute, that fat cow, that thrice-damned fool, that snake in the grass, that rotten slut, his former wife, had telephoned him from there. And if Italy exists, and Elizaveta was there, then he was simply obligated to curse the country in his next sermon. Without a doubt, Italy was a font of vice, and he'd fallen out of love with it, and with his wife, too, during that terrible night.

"A country of degenerate tarts and their gigolos! Den of depravity, Whore of Babylon!" he proclaimed in church.

The crowd, after listening to the sermon, dispersed silently.

And in the spring, Father Paisii began collecting money and packing his suitcases for a trip to Italy.

4

Serafim was awakened by a mysterious din in the distance. The drone wasn't very loud, but it was constant, persistent, menacing. Lazily drawing open his eyes, Serafim looked sadly at the room's whitewashed ceiling. A house. His house. In Larga. Some two weeks ago he thought he'd never wake up here again, now here he was ...

Sighing, Serafim extracted his feet from the down comforter he and his wife had received as a wedding gift and slapped them down onto the hideous carpet with a rooster pattern. His wife Marchika ran off with an agitator who gave lectures on atheism in 1987, but before that, she'd covered all the floors in the house with rugs like this. She was an irrepressible fan of the color red. Serafim sat for a while and once his feet got used to the cool floor, he distracted himself from his distressing thoughts and perked up his ears again. The din hadn't faded. It was an unusual noise for the village. Serafim had heard something similar once in Chisinau, when he'd walked by *Stadionul Republikan*, the national stadium.

"Serafim, how long can one man sleep?" shouted his bachelor neighbor, Old Man Tudor, through the open window. "Get to work, you lout, you."

Serafim got up. He had a soft spot in his heart for Old Man Tudor, who'd helped him, through conversation and advice, during the difficult period after his wife left. He threw off the blanket and went out into the yard. The sun, as if suffering from a hangover, was swaying unsteadily on the edges of the horizon, illuminating land that had contracted from the cold. "Like a baby in its mother's womb," thought Serafim. And he clenched his teeth. He and Marchika never had any children.

"Screw it," he blurted out halfheartedly, under the stern glance of Old Man Tudor. "Who cares about work, or the fact that yesterday I had a drop or two? Who cares about anything here? I'm leaving for Italy no matter what. As for this, it could all burn to the ground. Let the homestead crumble!"

Tudor looked at Serafim sternly. Serafim shivered and rinsed his face and torso with water that had partially frozen overnight. It was a practice his father taught him. "You put a bucket with well-water in the yard, and during the night the cold kills all the microbes, all the nastiness. The bits gets drawn into the ice," his old man told him. "And whatever hasn't frozen or fallen to the bottom— that's water for life! Bathe with it, rinse your mouth, and in twenty years you won't lose five teeth. Drink it, and flowers will grow in your heart. Pour it over your body, and your body'll turn green and pull itself upwards, just like a young poplar tree ..."

Serafim shook himself off and spit, recalling his forty-year-old father's rotten teeth, his stooping spine and his ever-present hand-rolled cigarettes, stuffed with unbearably smoky Moldovan tobacco. True, his dad always said it was hard work on the land that had killed him. And so he told his son, "Never give your all to this land. Think about how to get yourself out of here."

So Serafim came up with a plan: Italy. He'd go to Italy. To a country where the streets are always clean, the people are kind and pleasant, where without having to kill yourself you'd make in a month what you couldn't earn in three years of working the land in Moldova. Where the earth smells fresh, like pasta seasoning, where the sea is salty, warm and radiant, like the sweat of a woman you're lying on top of …

"Let the whole place burn, you say?" Old Man Tudor bit his lips sternly. "Well, it looks like the farm heard your plea. The earth's got a good grasp of the human mind."

Serafim looked around and smiled involuntarily. It really did look like the place had been overrun by the Turks. The picket fence surrounding the house had long ago begun to resemble his father's jaw, with slats missing here and there. And the modest attempts by the owner to conceal the gaps in the fence with shrubbery, while effective enough in the summer, were a complete fiasco in winter. The leaves fell off the trees and the fence looked even more pathetic. Neglected apple trees grew near the back entrance behind the house. The small pigsty for three or four hogs had long stood empty. Sometimes Serafim, coming home drunk and in no condition to fit his key into the lock, would lie down there and snore away, keeping warm in the thin, dusty straw where the pigs used to roll around. It seemed to Serafim that the straw still retained the warmth of the piggy bodies, just like his down comforter still retained the heat from the thighs of his licentious wife, Marchika. But owing to an odd weakness of his, and the bliss that gripped his body every time he cuddled up with his comforter, he couldn't bring himself to throw it out.

Usually the yard was full of mud, up to the knees, and in bad weather Serafim hopped through it from one rock to another, which he scattered around the house.

"This is that *whatsitcalled*," Old Man Tudor would laugh, scrunching his thin lips. He was smarter than he liked to look. "The Moldovan Stonehenge! And Serafim, that pancake, has gone and turned himself into a Druid."

Fortunately, the ground wasn't soft now. It had frozen and shrunk just like an abandoned child at a train station, and it was asking you to take it in your hands and warm

The Good Life Elsewhere

it with your breath.

"The land demands toil!" barked the thoughtful Tudor, standing near the fence. "So that's your plan, in the end?" he asked. "Italy, Shmitaly, without our cornstalks we won't be able to warm ourselves ..."

Serafim dutifully completed his morning ablutions, threw on a checkered cowboy shirt, and followed behind Tudor's bicycle, mumbling something on the way.

"I'm conjugating verbs," he admitted halfheartedly; he'd seen the surprised look on his crony's face. "What do you expect? I get no practice speaking it, so I might at least learn the grammar by heart."

Tudor nodded without saying a word. He began pedaling faster and faster. The din was louder now. Serafim and Tudor, intrigued, stepped up their respective paces and finally came to the edge of the village. Behind the last house, where there was a plateau about one square mile wide, they saw twenty villagers arrayed around a small, but genuine, podium. Serafim's acquaintance, Nikita Tkach, was standing on top of it, conducting. With every wave of his hand he shouted something out. The people who were gathered around him all piped up at once with a few phrases. Everybody was holding a book in his hands, which was even more surprising considering how what was left of the village library had perished ten years ago under the snow, wind, burning heat and rain. And these books seemed to be brand new. It didn't take the devil to see that some devilish plan was being hatched.

Serafim fell off the bicycle and Tudor just barely managed to catch him under the arm. The two men—one young, one old—froze in astonishment. The bicycle lay nearby, doubled up like an ancient Moldovan acacia. Its wheels went round and round, and from the grey sky's perspective, they recalled a potter's wheel with their pointless spinning ...

"The *stone*," cried Nikita Tkach—

"Is equipment used in the game," the choir glanced at their books and shouted, "weighing thirty-eight pounds and fourteen inches in diameter!"

Tkach raised his hand. "Attention! Exactly 38, and not 39, or, for example, 37! Be diligent with the details, got it?"

"Got it!!!"

"I'll go on," shouted Tkach. "The house. What is the *house*?"

"The house is a circle, 3.6 meters in diameter, where the stones are aimed," the gathered crowd called back at once.

"How about the *end*?" asked Nikita, with the intonation of the author of the Apocalypse.

"A period of the game during which the teams take turns sliding their 16 stones. Each game consists of 10 ends!" the listeners chanted.

"What's a *skip*?" asked Nikita trickily, with a squint.

"Not what, but who!" The villagers crowding the rostrum reproached their leader in a voice. "The skip is the captain of the team, he calls the shots."

"And the vice-skip?" Nikita asked a very easy question. "What's that?"

"Not what, but who!" the crowd answered, again with reproach and, of course, of one voice. "According to the rules, he's the player who has to stand at the other end of the curling sheet behind the house and help the skip call the shots!"

Two skylarks weaving a nest flew into the gaping mouths of Serafim and Old Man Tudor and deposited their young. Leaving the chicks to chirp, the birds flew off to the field for sustenance. It was getting cold now. The wheels of the fallen bicycle spun and spun. Nikita Tkach, catching sight of the observers on the sidelines out of the corner of his eye, puffed out his chest. The people stared at him adoringly. From a distance, it brought to mind the first Christians listening to their prophet or apostle and repeating after him. And these *were* the first Christians, in a way. Nikita sang them the praises of the City of God. More precisely, he talked about reaching it.

"Let's put aside the terminology," he shouted, leaning over the podium. "Listen to what I say. Remember, getting to Italy under the auspices of a tourism agency is a rotten business. We'll end up in the hands of swindlers, just like last time, and waste a lot of money again. Which we don't have, by the way. Isn't that right?"

"Uh-huh!" droned the crowd, approvingly.

"That means, we'll have to make sure they let us into Italy without any money. And who travels penniless, without anybody placing obstacles in their way? Who?"

"Tramps!" shouted out the village shepherd, Gitse. "Tramps and beggars!"

"True," nodded Nikita. "But so do diplomats and athletes!"

"So we're going to be diplomats?" asked Gitse, correcting himself.

"We're going to be athletes," said Tkach, correcting him, in turn. "And real ones, too. If we get the paperwork as a sports team and make it to Italy, the first policeman we come across is going to stop us. Because it'll be easy to figure out we're not athletes, won't it?"

"Yes," answered the audience.

"And we can't become a track team or a swim team, or, say, a boxing team, because the swimming, track and field and boxing federations have long been taking care of these issues, and they don't tolerate competition! Not to mention, we're neither swimmers nor runners nor boxers, right?"

"Right," the crowd obediently agreed. They were under Nikita's spell. "Absolutely ..."

"Though what *is* absolute?" sighed Nikita, who spent two years (the second and the fourth year) at veterinary school. "Nevertheless, I'll go on. And so, what we've got to do is choose a rare sport. Take it up. And play our way to Italy."

"Incredible!" The people were surprised at Nikita's intelligence.

"And in Italy this coming spring, only one sport will be having its championship," Nikita concluded. "The European Curling Championship. We have to make it. We have to win the elimination rounds, which are going to be in Moldova, Romania and Ukraine. We have to become the best curlers in the region!"

"Yes!!!"

"Curlers, and no fools allowed. No fools allowed in curling!"

"Yes-Yes-Yes!!!"

"And what do we need in order to do this?"

"A knowledge of the terminology and the rules. The ability to play. And the will!"

"One hundred percent," shouted Nikita. "Moldovans! Good people! Abandon your good-for-nothing fields, because your land yields naught. Throw down your plows and spades, shovels and hoes ... Abandon your wretched farms and sign up for my curling team, for this is your only chance to make it to the Promised Land, to Italy!"

"Yes!!!" Nikita's followers howled. They were mad with ecstasy.

"Which is exactly why I sent my last one hundred euros to Iasi, to buy thirty do-it-yourself guides to curling!" shouted Nikita. "Everything else, it's true, we'll have to make with our own hands. Everything, everything! The uniforms, the stones, the brooms! It won't be easy. Are you ready?"

"Yes!!!"

"And how! I'm ready too, because at the end of our hard work, what awaits us?"

"Italy!"

"I can't hear you!"

"I-ta-ly!"

"That's not what I want to hear from you," said Tkach, in ecstasy himself. "I want to know: What is a sweeper?"

"Not what," corrected the curling cult of Larga, who'd caught on to their leader's methodology, "but who! He's the player who sweeps the ice in front of the stone as it's sliding. Each team has two players at this position!"

"Yes!" howled Nikita. "And a draw?"

"A set-up shot, the goal of which is to place your stone in the house without touching the opponent's stones," the people sang out in unison.

"A take-out?" said Nikita, tilting his head back.

"A knock-out shot," the choir answered without hesitation, "with the goal of knocking the opponent's stone out of the house. At the same time, depending on which tactic you choose, your stone either stays in the house or goes out, too."

"A guard. Who's the guard?" said Nikita, being tricky again.

"Not who, but what!" A defensive stone, placed in front of the house and preventing the opponent from accomplishing his mission!!!"

The skylarks had fed their freshly-hatched nestlings with scarce and sleepy worms from the cool ground, and now they were thoroughly rinsing their feathers in Serafim's mouth. They began to chirp. Serafim was just coming back down to earth, and he carefully extracted the fledglings from his mouth. Tudor did the same. After they released the skylarks, the men watched silently as the birds somersaulted beneath the autumn sun. The skylarks bathed in its icy light like the ghosts of mermaids playing in the waning waters of the Prut River, beneath the mists.

"Our goal?" asked Nikita Tkach. "What is it, brothers?"

"Italy!" answered the villagers, in unison.

"Yes, but first, our goal is to master the game of curling," explained Nikita. "This will lead us to Italy. Our goal is to get the disk-like object with the handle across the ice into the finely drawn target! And so – what's our goal?"

"Our goal is to get the disk-like object with the handle across the ice into the finely drawn target!"

"Amen!" bellowed Nikita.

Finally, after tumbling through the air, the birds disappeared. Tudor picked up his bicycle. Its wheels had stopped spinning. Serafim silently lent a hand, and the men walked out onto the fields to gather the remains of the dry cornstalks so they'd have something to kindle the stove with in the darkness of the coming winter evenings.

The skylarks, meanwhile, flew off in search of other daydreamers.

The Good Life Elsewhere

5

Old Man Tudor and Serafim returned in the evening, tired and angry. The road ahead of them glimmered with the yellow-grey stalks of dried-up corn. In reality, there were no such stalks shimmering on the road, but the villagers couldn't help but imagine them wherever they looked. Just as the green sprouts of the tomato seedlings winked at them in spring and the grapevines sparkled green and blue in the summer.

"The fields aren't really shimmering," said Old Man Tudor. "It's the work itself that's dogging our every step."

Serafim kicked a can of Coca-Cola that had just been tossed from the window of a speeding car. "Stay put, you say. What awaits us here? Dirt, poverty, a whole lot of lousy nothingness. And how quickly everything went to pot. All in the twenty or so years since the Soviet Union fell apart."

"Under the Soviets, things were bad, too, it's just that you're young and you don't remember anything," said the old man, pedaling harder and barely opening his eyes. "But I remember. Dirt, poverty, and a whole lot of lousy nothingness have *always* been here."

"I've got to go to Italy," Serafim said.

"Italy, Italy, you keep chirping," said Tudor, getting angry. "Better you tell me this: Have you heard about Maria hanging herself?"

"Yeah," Serafim sighed. "When are they burying her?"

"First they've got to take her down."

"What? They haven't taken her down yet?"

"She's been hanging on the acacia tree for three weeks," the old man said sadly. "Her husband doesn't want to take her down. Her swaying body has a soothing effect on him, he says."

"Tfu," spit Serafim. "Inhuman."

"We're all human," admitted Tudor. "We're all people, we're all little persons. He should be pitied. The man's lost his tractor."

"His tractor is a piece of metal. We're talking about a human being!" said Serafim angrily.

"But for him, a tractor isn't simply a piece of metal. For him, it's everything. Just like Italy is for you," said Tudor, needling his young friend.

"And you dare compare them!" said Serafim, all worked up. "Italy is a beautiful country, easy work. Money, cleanliness, museums, paintings, pizza. And on the other hand, you've got a greasy tractor!"

Tudor was silent. Then, in a strained voice, he spoke up.

"Akh, Serafim, Serafim, you featherbrain. The wind blows in one ear and out the other. That's why Marchika left you. What does a woman need in life? She needs an anchor. A man made of steel, heavy, who doesn't doubt himself. And you've got a breeze blowing through your head. A breeze, and that Italy of yours."

"Alright, already—" Serafim tried to interrupt his friend, but Tudor was determined to finish.

"For a tractor driver, a tractor is his dream. Just like Italy is for you. That's what I mean. I'm comparing Italy to a dream. I'm not comparing Italy to a tractor. You see?"

"Yeah, yeah," nodded Serafim, not understanding a thing.

"There, there. And you immediately bring up nonsense."

The Good Life Elsewhere

The bicycle pulled up to the Lungu house and the men dismounted. Serafim walked behind the house to get a look at Maria, while Tudor politely but insistently knocked on the door. Vasily, with a yawn, stepped out of the house and skeptically looked over the visitors.

"You've come for my Maria?" he asked right away.

"For her," Tudor confirmed the purpose of the visit. "I brought some nuts ..."

An hour later a fire was blazing in the middle of the courtyard, and its shadows danced along the walls of the house. The walls were a mixture of clay, straw and horse manure. The men sat around the fire and lazily raked the walnuts out of the ashes with little sticks. With their fingers, stiff from working in the fields, they cracked them open, and the men ate the sweet hearts at the center. They drank down the sweet nuts with a sour wine. Maria had been a master wine presser.

"Maria was a master, she pressed the best wine for roasted nuts," said Tudor pensively. He drank from the glass, then passed it on to Vasily. "You can drink wine like this instead of the vitamins they sell at the pharmacy."

"You're not wrong," agreed Vasily. "Hear that, wife? The villagers are talking you up!" he shouted to the back of the house.

Serafim and Vasily snickered a little under the disapproving glance of Tudor, cleared their throats, and once again passed the wine around the circle. By their fourth liter, Serafim entered the game.

"You see," he said, looking pleadingly into Vasily's face, "other people nearby won't understand our village if they find out there's a corpse dangling in one of our backyards. They'll think we're apostates."

"We are apostates!" said Vasily sharply. "Even without a tractor," he added illogically.

"We'll buy you another tractor," said Serafim, trying

to comfort his fellow villager. "Once we're in Italy, we'll save up our money and buy one!"

"I've had it up to here with your Italy," snapped Vasily. "My wife chewed my ear off about it, too. And how did it all end? You got taken for a ride. And why? Well, because simple people always get made fools of. Dunces! Ah, pour me some more!"

"I give you my word," said Serafim, crossing himself, "I'll send you the money myself. Just let us bury Maria. Like a human being. As it is, she's hanging there turning everybody's blood cold. What do you need it for?"

"I guess I don't, really," admitted Vasily. "I've been thinking, I went too far when I said I'd never forgive her no matter what. I know a guy from the town of Alexeevca who's got an old beat up car. He promised to let me have it. It's got no motor. I'll fit it out with an engine, cook something up and turn it into a tractor."

"It turns out," sighed Old Man Tudor, "you did go too far."

"We went too far," Vasily repeated. "You hear that, Maria? We went too far with this hanging business!" he shouted into the night.

"Well, if it's like that, let's bury her," said Tudor thoughtfully. "It'll be quick. It's not as if you need her hanging there outside the house, do you?"

"Ah, no," said Vasily with a wave of his hand. "Dead or alive, she's of no use. Even the crows are scrambling to get into the garden, out of her sight, and they're not afraid of anything. Except … Oh, there's nothing to say. It's better to see something a hundred times, than hear it twice. Or how's the expression go? Anyway, let me show you."

Vasily got up from his seat and, a bit unsteady on his feet, ran into the cellar. Serafim and Tudor were sitting back to back, and they moved their pitchforks closer, just in case.

Tudor, to the same effect, heated the end of a fat metal rod in the fire so that, if anything happened, he could poke out drunk Vasily's eyes in a flash.

Here he was at last, running up from the cellar with a new jug of wine. He placed the jug on the ground, took a slug of it, and passed it around to his drinking buddies. They didn't bother with a glass anymore. The friends let their guard down and Vasily began his confession.

"At night," he said, raising a finger, "I hang strands of garlic on her to dry."

"Why not in the cellar?" asked Tudor stupidly.

"The air's stagnant down there. Up here there's some air," Vasily explained. "The body spins around in the breeze, and that's good, because garlic needs ventilation."

6

Toward February, the villagers of Larga decided to hold their first curling tournament. The ground was extremely warm and the already dried-up cornstalks were becoming even drier in the barns, waiting in anguish for the warm embrace of a fire. Owing to these circumstances, plus the lack of an ice rink in town, they decided to play on the simple dirt. The players dragged along a stone, until they put a sort of skateboard beneath it. Vasily the tractor driver had rigged it up. The game was starting at noon, and the crowd couldn't care less that Father Paisii, the village priest, had already cursed the whole mini-tournament, calling it a demonic delusion of a demonic Italy.

Nikita Tkach, dressed in his most stylish threads, addressed the villagers.

"Train like a grunt, conquer like a general. The bullet flies but a sword never lies. You want to go to Italy, don't put the cart before the … I mean, you've got to push that stone! Are you ready?"

"Ready!" shouted the players.

The whistle blew and the game was on. True, the curlers from Larga were supposed to be playing with a forty-five pound stone. The stone they had weighed an unofficial three hundred pounds, give or take; the Largans decided to train in the most difficult conditions in order to achieve maximal effectiveness. This way, they'd qualify for the international tournament for sure.

Nikita watched the players from the tribune he'd knocked together himself with no small excitement. Every minute or so, Tkach would gargle water in his throat from a dusty decanter he'd found in the village general store a few years back. The decanter was cracked but the spider web of fractures along its thick side only made the vessel appear more graceful, like a touch of grey on the temples of a respected elder. The decanter and his glass clinked as they touched, and so did Nikita Tkach's heart when he saw the first ever curler in the village of Larga launch the first ever curling stone in the village of Larga across the field during the first ever curling tournament in the village of Larga ...

"Launching the stone!" the attacker shouted, and with a running start he began pushing the stone in front of him. "Step aside!"

The players on one team carefully swept the ground in front of the stone with actual brooms, stand-ins for real curling equipment. Theoretically, they were smoothing the ice the imagined stone was supposed to spin on, to make it go quicker. The attackers labored on, but the stone didn't spin any faster. In fact, the brooms were merely furrowing the ground.

"The brooms are furrowing the ground!" one of the players shouted to Nikita. He was getting under Nikita's skin, pestering him with leading questions. "The brooms are supposed to smooth out the ice, not tear it up!"

"Keep on smoothing out the ground!" warned Tkach.

"How am I supposed to smooth it out if—" The annoying player glanced at his broom with surprise. It was laced with nails.

Nikita filled his lungs with air so he could mock the ignoramus. He would have explained that the brooms had been *specially* laced with nails to make the game even harder. But he didn't have time, because a minute later, there was nobody to explain anything to.

"Smooth out the ground with a broom that's laced

with nails?" the player had said, surprised. "That's im-poss—"

And then he died, felled by the stone that had fallen off the wooden board. In the ensuing silence Nikita took a swig of air from the glass (since it was empty and Tkach had forgotten to refill it) and slowly made his way down toward the stone. Brownish blood trickled out from underneath it, mixing with the earth.

He didn't suffer much," somebody hesitantly offered.

"We have to check. We might be able to save him. Although …" A voice in a hoarse whisper was coming from the rear of the assembly.

"Don't remove the stone," decided Nikita. "He'll lie here like a submarine at the bottom of the sea."

The players took off their hats for a moment of silence.

Father Paisii, as a priest of the Moldovan Metropolitan of the Orthodox Church, refused to sing the requiem.

However, as a priest of the Bessarabian Metropolitan, which in no way at all recognized the authority of the Moldovan Metropolitan, Paisii performed it.

7

IN THE OLD DAYS, WHEN THE VILLAGERS WERE MORE OR less contented and hadn't begun dreaming about Italy, Larga was known all over Moldova for two major attractions.

The first was a trolley park.

The first trolley appeared in Larga in 1970, ten years before the appearance of the Ferris wheel. The trolley park came about because the region was the country's leader in the cultivation of aromatic plants. And for that, it received a prize of fifteen million rubles.

"Fifteen million rubles to the region," said the chairman of the collective farm, holding the congratulatory telegram in his trembling hand. "And nearly a million is earmarked for our village!"

After the announcement, many of the villagers lapsed into deep thought. What to spend the money on? They all had to decide together. On the one hand, this simplified the task; on the other hand, it made it much harder.

"If we use the money to buy a tractor, it'll be Vasily's lucky break, but what about the rest of us?" This was overheard in one of the courtyards.

"If we buy feed or seed," they said in the park, "then we'll be giving all our money to the government again. And how long can we keep fluffing their pillows?"

"No way they're building a cowshed!" they decided at the town club. "The chairman's daughter is the chief milker. Why should we give her a present?"

"Road construction?" said somebody else, skeptically.

"What would that do for us?"

Which is why nobody had any immediate objections at the meeting when Dygalo, the village idiot who moonlighted as an agronomist with a PhD in Agricultural Sciences, suggested the following:

"Hey, let's put a trolley in town!"

The suggestion only seemed silly at first glance. After some thought, it was thoroughly appealing. Indeed, installing a trolley wouldn't give anybody a pretext for jealousy. It wouldn't put a feather in anybody's cap. It wouldn't improve anybody's life. Everyone was satisfied.

"From the collective budget, the community has decided to buy a trolley, build a track, and pay the trolley driver's salary," they announced in Larga.

A month later a trolley, with a completely insane driver from Chisinau, was rolling through Larga, which was all of two miles long. The driver had been exiled to the provinces for comporting himself poorly at party meetings. There were three stops on the trolley line, and at the end they built an improvised trolley park comprising a massive barn, a booth for the dispatcher and bookkeeper, and benches for the controller and the conductor. The "bus with horns"—that's what they called the trolley— ran strictly according to schedule. Once every half hour. The dubiousness of the situation didn't bother anybody.

"It is marvelous that in the villages of the Republic the people are pushing toward progress in every sphere," they announced in Chisinau.

Little by little the villagers got used to the trolley. In 1976, the first trolley pickpocket appeared in the village! The "asocial element" Petra Ivantsok specialized in the theft of valuables at rush hour. Since everybody knew that Petra was the only pickpocket in town, the passengers gave him a daily beating, dragging him from the trolley at rush hour. Thanks to which, Petra went to pieces, became a physical and spiritual invalid, and in 1980 he wrote a letter to the Central Committee of the Communist Party of the Soviet Union requesting recognition as a "veteran of labor," along with an honorific and a larger pension.

Surprisingly, they granted his request. Petra received an increased pension for nearly two years before the Department of Letters at the Central Committee got smart to the situation. And when they did figure it out—in order to avoid drawing attention to their mistake—they decided to increase Petra's pension yet again.

Little by little, Ivantsok, the only resident of Larga whose fate had been improved by the trolley, fell into senile dementia and started telling the village teenagers all sorts of tales about his heroic past; he started believing them himself. He took over the reins from Dygalo, the village idiot who moonlighted as an agronomist with a PhD in Agricultural Sciences. Dygalo had died five years earlier; he was never able to bounce back from the injury of hearing about Ivantsok's personal pension. So Petra gradually took Dygalo's place in the life of the village.

In 1980 the region became the all-Moldova champion in tobacco harvesting, surprising even itself. For this, the government of the Republic awarded the region twenty million rubles. The chairman, his hair gone grey thanks to this second blow of fateful luck, again went to the people.

The telegram was quivering slightly in his hands like a lone, fallen leaf at twilight on the autumn plow lands along the Dniester.

"Twenty million rubles," said the chairman, "and nearly two million of it is earmarked for Larga ..."

If it had taken place today, the villagers would have immediately decided to spend the money on relocating themselves to Italy. But back then life was merely bad, not terrible. And so the people went back to their homes despondent. Solving the problem would be even thornier than last time. After all, they already had a trolley. What to spend the money on? And how to do it without ruffling any feathers?

Nobody objected at the meeting when Petra Ivantsok, the village idiot who moonlighted as the former pickpocket of Larga and personal pensioner of the government of the USSR, suggested the following:

"Hey, why don't we build an amusement park in the village with a huge Ferris wheel?!"

Thus, Larga acquired its second major attraction.

In time, of course, both the trolley park and the amusement park fell into disrepair. People carried off the passenger cars from the Ferris wheels to their homes, turning them into outdoor pavilions. Old Man Tudor enterprisingly installed the horse from the children's carousel as a weathervane on the roof of his house. Never mind that the horse was heavy and didn't turn with the wind. The chains from the chair swing ride were snatched up by mechanics from the surrounding villages for use on their farms.

Girls whispered into each other's ears, giggling and turning red: "You wouldn't believe what goes on at night at the top of the Crazy Biker ride ..."

After the Soviets lost power in Moldova, a priest was assigned to the village. Father Paisii cursed the rides as the devil's playground and placed an ironclad ban on Orthodox Christians entering the territory of the former amusement park. He grandiosely set fire to the remains of the Ferris wheel. Seeing how the passenger cars had already been carried off, nobody missed the wheel ...

"As for the trolley park," decided Paisii, back then still entirely content with his Elizaveta, her milky thighs showing through the slit of her chemise, "we'll let it be, if you please. We'll adapt the trolley for the needs of the

Almighty."

According to Paisii's plan, they could transport miracle-working icons across the village on the trolley and ask God now for rain, now for sun, depending on which catastrophe at any given time was preventing the peasants from gathering their imaginary harvests. Many grumbled and said that under the Soviets, there was no prayer, but a harvest there had been.

"That's because under the Soviets we sold our souls to the devil. In return he granted us the devil's harvest," the young and ambitious priest explained.

The argument was flawless and self-assured and nobody raised an objection. The trolley bore three Cross Processions, after which it became clear to everyone that besides the devil's harvest, the accursed Soviet powers had also provided the village with electricity aplenty. Without that, it turned out, the trolley couldn't run.

"Then we'll push it," said Paisii enthusiastically, since in any case, he wouldn't be the one to roll up his sleeves. "The Lord will help!"

The Cross Processions became a tradition in Larga.

Paisii, who hated taking walks since childhood, was put out. True, nowadays he'd agree to a hundred, two hundred, a thousand Processions a year. If it would bring his wife back, he'd get a gardening job in Italy. With only a remote idea about gardening, Paisii thought it would be breezy, no-sweat work, and plus he'd have his wife and kids at his side. Where? In Italy, of course. After all, so the gossip went, it was paradise. Now, if he could just figure out how to scrape up the four thousand euros he needed. For the only valuable item in the church, the miracle-working icon of Nikolai the Passion Bearer, the priest had gotten just five hundred euros. The Chisinau pawnbrokers wouldn't accept the church building as a deposit. The fact that it was a church wasn't what gave them pause.

Paisii knew for certain that others had pawned churches for credit towards a vacation, apartment, or their education. A few banks had even pooled their resources and started an advertising company aimed at extending credit to Moldovan men of the cloth.

Paisii keenly recalled his humiliation as he went from pawnshop to pawnshop, and repeated to himself the argument the brokers had made when refusing him. Standing at the window, black with despair and nighttime, he whispered:

"The church, you see, has no *liquidity* ..."

8

NOT FAR FROM THE AMUSEMENT PARK, A PAIR OF STORKS rested atop the roof of a house and calmly looked each other over. Nearby sat two men: a stovemaker and the owner of the house.

"Put your hand on the chimney," said the stovemaker.

"It's hot! I'll burn myself," said the owner reluctantly. "The smoke ..."

"Touch it!!" shouted Eremei.

The owner cautiously brought his hand close to the chimney. Gathering his courage, he made contact. Then, laughing with surprise, he thrust his hand inside the chimney all the way to his elbow.

"It's cool!" he blurted out in amazement. "The smoke is completely cool!"

"Like ice," smiled Eremei. "Like real, cold ice. There it is. Put your hands on it, feel it. If you can touch it, it means it's real."

For Eremei, the stovemaker from Alexeevca, the world was divided in two halves: the real and the invented. Alexeevca, Eremei himself (whom he could touch with his own hands), his tools, tile stoves, his wife Lida, his daughter Evgenia, the grass in the fields, the land, the well where the sun went down in the evenings and in the morning struggled out to dry off and spin in the sky – all these belonged to the first category. In the category of invented things, Eremei, who didn't much go for philosophy, placed what he considered to be paranormal phenomena.

Things like ghosts, honest state agronomists, an Olympic victory for the Moldovan team in the upcoming games in China in 2008 and … Italy.

"It doesn't exist. There's no such thing as Italy," he categorically declared as he made his rounds. He'd dramatically smack his trowel against the clay, keeping rhythm with his own argument. "The whole thing was invented by international swindlers!"

"What do you mean?" the educated folks would ask in surprise. "Italy's right there on the map."

"Give me a map, I'll draw anything you want on it," coughed Eremei. "Of course the country exists. But it's obvious they don't need our workers there. It's all just an elaborate scheme."

Eremei would explain himself to the gaping public who often gathered in the village to listen to the stovemaker. He was a well-respected man. "They say all sorts of things. They claim two hundred thousand Moldovans have already gone there, but tell me, has anybody here ever seen this place they call Italy?

One of the listeners timidly spoke up. "My neighbor told me that his cousin's son from Marculesti went to Italy. Every month he sends them two hundred euros!"

But Eremei made a mockery of the bickering villager by suggesting the young man from Marculesti had long ago been sold for his organs. The group gasped and Eremei went about building the stove like an old hand. He loved to chat while he worked, like an ancient Russian storyteller singing a folk song.

"It's obvious. These swindlers, they make a heap of money selling dead bodies," he said, lifting his trowel. "And one of the con men's got half a conscience. So he sends some crumbs back to the boy's parents."

"What do you mean, crumbs?" they said. They were trying to trip up Eremei with his own words. "We're talking about two hundred euros!"

"For us it's a banquet," Eremi laughed, "but for them, it's crumbs."

The villagers became sadly silent, picturing the kind of wealth that makes two hundred euros seem like crumbs. Eremei put down his trowel and went to eat lunch. He always ate at home, but picked up his conversation when he returned as if there hadn't been a nearly hour-long interruption.

"Of course, I don't think they sold two hundred thousand Moldovans' organs in Italy," he said, softening up after lunch like any man. "Some must have survived. I bet they're being held in captivity and forced to work. Their captors are making millions off them ... No, billions! And so they send some crumbs to the relatives."

"But why go that far?" asked the owner of the house where Ermolai was working. "The swindlers can exploit the Moldovans either way."

"This way, nobody asks too many questions," answered the stovemaker. He'd already thought about it, and now he took a minute to bask in the effect his words were having on the villagers.

And there really was an effect. Eremei was not only an unpredictable, witty and original orator,—the village teacher on his deathbed had called Eremei the Cicero of Alexeevca—he was also a superb stovemaker. Legends were constructed about his stoves. Everyone knew the smoke that came out of a stove made by Eremei always came out cold. This meant, he diverted *all* the heat from the fire inside the home. Many times his rivals tried to see exactly how the stovemaker complicatedly arranged the flue; each time they simply became confused, crying bitterly and gnashing their teeth at their own impotence. And why wouldn't they? One stove cost nearly two hundred leu, or twenty euros. That was reason enough to consider Eremei a man of substance. Such substance, in fact, that thieves broke into his house on more than one occasion. But they never found anything and left empty-handed.

"Where do you hide the money so well that nobody ever finds it?" the stovemaker's wife asked him after one unsuccessful robbery attempt.

"Look over here." Eremei mysteriously beckoned to Lida and raised his finger. "Not a word to anybody."

It turned out Eremei kept all his valuables in the stove, directly underneath the flame. But he'd designed the stove so brilliantly that the place where the flame blazed was always cold. Lida, in awe of her husband's intelligence, thanked God for sending her such a good man and went to work in the fields. Eremei counted his money one more time and laid it under the flame without burning himself. This was his second secret, which he never even told his wife: fire had no power over him, it only brushed his skin like a cat's tongue licks the hand of a loving owner. Then the stovemaker righted himself, remembered Italy, which was the only thing people were talking about, and snorted. He heard footsteps.

"Papa," said his daughter, coming up behind him. "Lend me four thousand euros. I want to go work in Italy."

9

AFTER THE STORIES ABOUT PLANTING TREES IN BALTI, THE shooting of homeless dogs in Soroca, and the prime minister's press conference, it was time for a story about Italy on the local news.

"According to information from the Italy-Moldova Institute for Cooperation and Growth, the number of Moldovan citizens working illegally in Italy could reach two hundred thousand. The chairman of the Institute, Doina Babenko, announced on Tuesday that they are undertaking measures to support Moldovans working illegally in Italy, but according to …"

The nasal voice of the newscaster on Moldovan TV blabbed on.

Annoyed, Eremi turned off the set and paced the room, hands stuffed in his pockets. It was a little awkward these days for Eremei to debunk the myth of Italy. His daughter, after all, was working in Bologna. It was surprising, but Zhenya had made it to Italy, called once she got there, and said she'd been set up with a job. She was slowly paying back the debt to her parents. As it turned out, Italy *did* exist. At least that's what Eremei wanted to believe. Otherwise, he'd have to admit that the international mafia of human organ traffickers was sending him money after they'd sawed his daughter to pieces. Besides, Zhenya called regularly to report on what she was eating, how she was living, and to assure her parents that she wasn't smoking and everything was great. Eremei was happy—he loved his daughter—but since her departure he'd withdrawn into himself and become gloomy. It wasn't the separation from his daughter that was to blame.

"So, Eremei, there's no such thing as Italy, eh? Isn't your daughter there now? Maybe she doesn't exist either, ah?"

The stovemaker was badgered by friendly heckling. In his distress, he not only lost weight, he even stopped sleeping. His work was uneven, nervous. Eremei wasn't making mistakes, but a lot of people noticed that the smoke from his stoves had started coming out a bit warm. The stoves weren't retaining all the heat for the houses and the people inside. Some spiteful critics even conducted an experiment. They drove to the regional center and stole a thermometer from the local medical clinic. Then they slipped the device into the chimney of a house where Eremei had built the stove after his daughter's departure. A day later they fished out the thermometer.

"Thirty five degrees," announced the village's other stovemaker, Anatol Tkachuk, grandiosely.

The smoke from Anatol's stoves still came out seventy degrees Fahrenheit, as hot as a June afternoon. Clients didn't exactly flock to him. But everybody in town understood that Eremei was getting old. The master was losing his skills.

"Listen, Eremei," Postolika the farmer said to his friend Eremei sympathetically. "Why not just admit you were a bit off the mark when you said there's no such thing as Italy. I mean, people aren't animals. They'll understand. They'll forgive you. They might stop teasing you, too."

"People aren't the problem," admitted Eremei. "*I'm* the problem. You see, it's as though everything around me is collapsing. It turns out all these years I've been telling people tales …"

The townsfolk became more convinced about Eremei when rumors started circulating that Zhenya, his daughter, was coming from Italy to visit her parents. It was a special event. Up until now the most contact there had been between Moldovans in Italy and their relatives back at home were telephone conversations and money transfers. Eremei painstakingly prepared for his daughter's visit and even built a portable fireplace in her honor. True, the smoke came out—just a little—on the warm side.

Lida, the stovemaker's wife, exited the house on tiptoes and set off to drown herself. But Eremei knew the nearby river was a half-meter deep at its max and that his wife, a strong swimmer, could never drown in it. Too bad. "I wouldn't mind drowning, either," thought the stovemaker, but I haven't got the strength." He had reason to despair. Their daughter had arrived at the train station like a princess, all decked out and with loads of cash. But after meeting Zhenya there, her parents couldn't rejoice over her visit. Not after she told them what she'd been doing. And to all her mother's howling and the unspoken anger in her father's glance, she shouted maliciously, "So what? All of our people over there are doing the same thing. At least the younger ones. And even if you don't sell yourself openly, either way you're going to sleep with your boss if he says he wants it. What else am I supposed to do? Go home? To where? You call this a home? You've never seen a real home. This isn't a home – this is trash, a hole in the world, eternal humiliation! Moldova! Chisinau's alright enough, but if you want to live there you've got to have money for an apartment, right? And where are you going to find that here?"

She was just like her father: she spoke every harsh word with painstaking precision, the way Eremei would fit a tile onto the stove so that it was solid and plumb. And with each of his daughter's words, his spine stood straighter and straighter, though he realized there was no escaping the shame.

"What am I supposed to do here?" continued Zhenya. "I hate this trash, I hate everything in this place! It's all so depressing and nasty!"

Her mother sobbed, the stovemaker stared gloomily at the flame, and the daughter went to bed. Lida went off to drown herself, but an hour later she came back from the river, wet and tearful. Eremei gave his wife some motherwort tea, which put her to sleep like a child, and he sat in Zhenya's bedroom before dawn. For a long time he feasted his eyes on his daughter's wretched face. She had wronged them, but they loved her terribly.

And when the sun came up Eremei strangled his daughter and burned her body in his mightiest stove, where he usually forged tools for the machinists. He burned not only her body, but her ashes, too. When Lida woke up around noon, he told her their daughter had left of her own volition. And of course his wife was surprised, but she was so weak and disheartened she couldn't talk about it. With time, her doubts about Zhenya's departure faded and her faith in her husband was renewed. Even when he said that Italy didn't exist. And in the village, too, they believed him. What's not to believe? After all, Eremei the skeptic's daughter was supposed to come for a visit, and it seemed like she never had. Even the phone calls from Italy had come to a halt.

By summertime Eremei had built another stove. This one burped out puffs of the coldest, blackest smoke you've ever seen. And in contrast to Italy, you could touch it with your own hands.

"Fifteen degrees," they announced grandly at a village gathering. "Freezing!!!"

10

Mingir, a village in the Hincesti region, was famous throughout Moldova for its residents who habitually trafficked in kidneys. What's more, the kidneys were their own. There were already thirty such people in the town. Once in a while a correspondent for the BBC, Radio Liberty or *Der Speigel* would come to town, since every six months their bosses would demand a scandal. So they'd do a story on Mingir. For a bottle of cognac, reporters filled each other in on the town and its main attractions: there was Vasily Myrzu, who'd sold both kidneys at the same time for three thousand dollars and a Soviet clunker; Georgii Styncha, who traded his kidney for a horse and four hundred pounds of oats, and many others. The villagers lived in poverty, and what's more, they lived in pain. As the doctors say, without a kidney you're headed downstream ...

The old timer Jan Sandutsa gave a wink to his friend. "Predictions are for fortunetellers, Sunrise. The world is in for another surprise when they see how a simple Moldovan outfoxed them all. That's what our people've always stood for, and always will: street smarts and cunning. What do you say, pal?"

Jan's friend looked at him approvingly, but didn't say anything. In any case, he couldn't have: Sunrise was a pig, and pigs can't talk. At least not when they're being watched. But that didn't bother Jan. He viewed Sunrise from a strictly practical point of view: as an organ donor.

It all started in 1999 when one fine day some visitors from

Israel came to town. The guests, two of whom claimed to be doctors, convinced the villagers to put their kidneys up for sale. Everyone knew it was a raw deal, since two years earlier four Mingir residents had sold their kidneys and instead of the eight thousand euros they'd been promised, they each walked away with just three grand. The villagers knew: out-of-towners are swindlers! They unanimously decided not to give in to temptation and to sell their kidneys no more.

But late at night, one by one, fourteen souls in all, the villagers crept into the house where the Israeli troublemakers were sleeping. Among the creepers was old Jan.

They were all taken to Romania that same month for an operation. Old Jan woke up to the smell of ether, just like Doctor Zhivago atop a bed sheet white as an early spring snowfield. But Jan had never read *Doctor Zhivago*, so to him, ether was just ether. Someone shoved crinkled banknotes in his hand, dragged him out of bed, sent him unsteadily packing and slammed the door in his face.

"Four thousand euros!" said the old timer ecstatically. He was seeing double. He counted the bills in his hands right there on the street, not afraid of anything, seeing how he was still under the influence of the ether. "But they promised eight. They nearly robbed me blind!"

Once he emerged from his drug-induced fog, the old timer realized that his eyes really were seeing double, and the money was less than he thought: two thousand euros. But even that was pretty good! Glancing at the grubby cockroaches milling around the passengers' feet at the Bucharest railroad station, Jan mentally crossed himself and sang a hosanna to the Lord. Who was, without a doubt, from Moldova.

"Of course, God's Moldovan. Otherwise why would he give me so much help?" Jan whispered.

Just then, a policeman walked up and fined him three hundred euros for who-knows-what, which the old timer coughed up so as not to lose his entire stash. Jan realized that God is not only Moldovan, but also in some sense Romanian, too. The contradiction resolved itself when Jan recalled the close blood ties between the two nations.

He forfeited fifty euros to the conductor for a place in the luggage rack on the train to Chisinau. He greased the palm of a Moldovan customs agent with fifty big ones, and another hundred went to three glowering toughs at the Chisinau train station who were demanding money from all the arriving passengers. The station was dark and the policemen were still sleeping, so old Jan prudently decided to pay. At home he counted what remained of his money and crossed himself for the nth time that day.

"Fifteen hundred euros!" gasped Jan quietly. "Enough for a lifetime!"

In three months, the old timer had paid for his grand-daughter's wedding, the christening party of his nephew twice-removed, and buried his sister. The money had run out. Jan's back pain grew worse. In one year's time Jan had aged ten, and he went to Chisinau to get himself an artificial kidney. As a recipient of the Veteran of Labor medal, he thought the government ought pay for it. In Chisinau they laughed at the old man and advised him to buy a coffin and a cemetery plot. Back in the village, Jan spent the pension he hadn't touched in half a year ordering all sorts of medical literature.

At the post office he lied and told them he was trying to get into medical school. Everyone was quick to rag on him.

"Keep laughing, you chumps," he whispered, gripping the weighty packet of books in his arms, "This old tim-er here'll be laughing at you when I get my two kidneys again, both healthy and strong. When you're pushing up daisies, I'll still be here to mow the lawn!"

The old man was planning to get his kidney back in

an unusual way. Somewhere he'd heard that animal organs could be transplanted to humans, so he decided to transplant a kidney. In choosing a beast for this honorable mission, he settled on a pig. As the well-informed Jan already knew, pig organs were very similar to human ones. True, there was a "but"…

"People who receive transplants from pigs sometimes acquire the physical characteristics of these animals," a quack in a lab coat had mentioned on the TV program *Health*. "Such are the results of my many years of experiments. I conducted one experiment with our biological ancestors, monkeys, involving the transplant of various pig organs. Afterwards, in some monkeys we observed a change in behavior toward porcine habits. Specifically, they became less discriminating in what they ate. They began to gorge themselves on anything and everything. I postulate that something similar can happen with human beings."

Jan the old timer very nearly despaired. Then he got to thinking, it's better to be a living dirty pig than a dead gentlemen. The enterprising retiree undertook an inspection of his personal means and, combining the capital from his pension with the money he brought in by selling his last sack of corn, Jan bought a piglet.

"I'll call you Sunrise, since you symbolize a new life," he said proudly to the sweet little piglet oinking around the small pigsty. "Just as the sunrise conquers the night, your kidney will postpone my death and prolong my life!"

Unsuspecting of his noble purpose, Sunrise happily gobbled up the buckets of slops the old timer gave him and dropped off to sleep. He liked it in Jan's pigsty. The old man fed him well enough, and on top of that, he let the pig drink wine.

"Why not?" Jan reasoned to himself. "I'm going to be using the damn thing's kidney. Might as well get him used to my usual portion while he's still a youngin."

Sadly, the piglet never learned to smoke Jan's crude cigarettes, but he did guzzle wine with pleasure. Jan's future kidney was clearly acclimatizing with no problems. This made Jan happy. In time, the piggy boy became a piggy man. Everything was going according to plan. Only a few details remained. The most important one, Jan understood, was to cut open Sunrise's belly without harming the kidney. And then – the transplant. Jan liked to dream about this moment while he stood there, watching Sunrise at dawn.

"As for the kidney, I'll slip it in there myself. No big deal. I'll drink a hundred grams of vodka. As an *anesthewhatever*. It'll give me courage. I'll make the incision and slip it in. It'll grow fast. Christ, the body's no fool. It feels and understands. I mean, bones grow along with people!"

The old timer understood the risk was great but he had no choice. An operation cost an absurd amount of money, and the only place to get one done was in Switzerland. Even if the old man sold another of his kidneys, the money would just be enough for a preliminary medical exam. He could only count on himself. And on Sunrise.

One morning in June, Jan realized the time had come. Notwithstanding the chill in the air, the day promised to be impossibly hot. Nary a cloud floated across the sky, blue as the cobalt teapot belonging to Jan's wife. With each day Jan grew weaker. As the doctors explained, it was especially taxing to be in the heat with only one kidney. Patting Sunrise on the snout, the old man fed the hog no more. He didn't want to strain the kidney. Right there in the barn he began preparing for the operation, which would take place in the evening. He put a decanter of strong moonshine (from up north, near Balti) and two glasses on a table he brought in. There wouldn't be anybody to drink with, but to have only one glass would be somehow inhuman. Jan spread a towel across the table and took out a jar of pickles, to help the medicine go down. Then, he took out an expertly sharpened knife and undertook to slaughter Sunrise.

"So long, friend." Showing no emotion, the old timer quickly slashed the pig's throat. "Hello, kidney!" The pig, expecting breakfast, was unsuspecting.

And with a mighty blow he pricked the convulsing, dying Sunrise in the heart. The hog twitched a while longer then went still. The old man carefully extracted the pig's kidneys and laid them in the icebox. He threw the carcass in there too, so the meat wouldn't spoil. According to the scientific literature on the subject, the kidneys had to cool off now. You couldn't transplant them warm. After washing his hands, Jan crossed himself and went to work in the fields. In the evening, when the heat had fallen off, he walked past his house and headed straight for the barn. He picked up the knife, took a deep breath, drank a glass of moonshine, picked up the knife again, exhaled and stabbed himself smack in the side. Pressing the wound with his hands, he ran to the icebox and ... couldn't find the kidneys.

"Jan," his wife Anastasia yelled to him from the doorway. "Come inside this minute. I cooked up those kidneys you carved out. They're still warm. Come quick! You'll lick your fingers clean! Jan! What the ... Jan, what's wrong? Jan!"

Leaking blood, guts and tears, the old timer was crawling toward Anastasia so he could stab her, too, but halfway there, in the middle of the yard, he died. The autopsy revealed that Jan Sandutsa, b. 1927, died from shock and loss of blood, but both kidneys were in place.

However, his gallbladder, half of his liver, one lung, two heart ventricles and for some reason his appendix had all gone missing...

11

THE WINNING ENTRY IN THE RECIPE CONTEST AT *MOLDOVA Suverena* (Sovereign Moldova), timed for International Women's Day on March 8, was a letter from the Hincesti region. The result was even more remarkable since the very same item had also won the newspaper's literary contest, for being the most lyrical letter from a reader.

"Take two pork kidneys, a spoonful of vegetable shortening, two cups bouillon, 1/3 cup moonshine strong as a man's heart, plus half an apple, a tablespoon of flour white as a shroud, and a touch of antifreeze, to taste," wrote the reader Anastasia Sandutsa.

"Steep the kidneys in five cups of water," Anastasia wrote, "like a newborn baby in the tears of your heart. Rub salt into them as you would into the wounds of your heart after recalling an offense, and let them gather pity in the kitchen. Don't forget to cover them with cheesecloth. When the second hour chimes, sentence them to death or baptism, depending on your perspective. Drown them in clean water. Drown them without remorse, for they will be resurrected in the deluge of boiling water on the burner. When they are boiled and become as soft as you were a week before your wedding, ruthlessly cut them with a knife sharp as fury, cold as ice, grey as steel.

"Spread the bits of boiled kidney on a plate, just as the bones of the innocents who were put to death by Herod the Great were scattered around Jerusalem. Weep over them and do not suppress the sorrow in your heart. Better to light a candle and scorch the fresh greens with the flame to kill any disease. For there is baptism by fire or baptism by water, but baptism by fire is quicker.

"And while the kidneys cool, prepare the sauce," continued Anastasia Sandutsa, from the village of Minzhir in the Hincesti region, in her letter as sad as the cries of a little shepherd girl from the folk legends. "It will be thick as a river in high water, pungent as the foul smells from the farthest regions of your body …

"Anoint the saucepan with a touch of sunflower seed oil. Grease its scars, and as soon as the oil heats up, sprinkle with flour, pour on the bouillon and the moonshine strong as the heart of a village man who knows not how to love with his words, only with his actions, and add the chopped apple.

"When the sauce begins to bubble, add the kidneys and let them swim, let them cool, let them melt away.

"And then," wrote Anastasia, "kiss your own hand for cooking so well, and burst into tears.

"And since there is nobody who might devour it while singing your praises, who might eat it up so greedily, barely noticing the hints of flavor – eat it tenderly, eat it by yourself."

The reader's first submission was called "Recipe for kidneys in a strong sauce." The second – "Cry for your beloved husband, who left you." Having been chosen the winner, Anastasia received—for both contests—one first prize.

A live pig.

12

It was business as usual at the Italian Consulate in Romania. Five secretaries in the large, spacious premises painted their lips and caught sunbeams off their lacquered nails. From time to time they cut short this amusing activity and took up some documents. They separated the visa requests from Moldova and Romania; the ones from Romania they reviewed, but the Moldovan requests they stamped with a seal that said, "DENIED."

Consul Paolo Michelangelo Buonarotti ran his hand through his hair.

"Surprising, but true. Not a single Moldovan citizen gets a visa these days allowing him to stay in our country, let alone tourist or work visas. Still, we've got two hundred thousand Moldovans. You've been informed of the scale of the phenomenon, my friend?"

"My cook is from Moldova," answered the grey-haired man softly. He was of average height, with sad eyes; he looked like a detective in an eighties mafia movie. "A woman from Moldova takes care of my paralyzed aunt, and the street I live on is being paved by illegal Moldovan workers."

"That's how it is." Buonarroti slapped his colleague on the knee, causing him to pucker up his face. "They're like spiders. They've invaded and now you can't do anything about them."

"Absolutely true."

"Poor Italy."

"You're right."

"My hair stands up on end when I think about the

Russians."

"We're not at war with them again, are we?"

"No, no. What I mean is, the poor Russian have twice as many Moldovans as we do. Four hundred thousand!"

"Ooo-la-la."

"What are you, French?"

"On my mother's side. Does that bother you?"

"Not in the least. So these poor Russians have it a lot worse than us."

"Yeah, really. Those poor bastards."

"On the other hand, there are a lot more Russians than there are Italians. And in relation to their effect on the soul of the population, maybe we don't have fewer Moldovans after all."

"Could be."

"So those Russians aren't such poor bastards, after all."

"Absolutely true."

"Maybe we're even worse off than they are. What do you think?"

"I agree with you absolutely."

"What's sickening is that Moldovans seem to think without them we'll sink, because, as one cheeky laborer told me, there'll be nobody to clean up our shit."

"Bull's-eye!"

"What?

"I mean, *your* observations hit the bull's-eye, not the Moldovan's insolent baloney."

"Thank you. I told him that nature doesn't abide vacuums. Where there used to be two hundred thousand Moldovans, now there'll be two hundred thousand Moroccans, Albanians, Serbs, Poles, or whoever else. There's always somebody to clean up the shit. What's your opinion?"

"I'm struck by the depth and precision of your comments."

"Beasts ..."

"Did you deny this knuckledragger a visa?"

"Naturally. How he scored himself an interview at all, I can't understand. There's a directive to deny everyone at the initial stage."

"Seems to me, that's fair."

The consul offered his colleague a Gauloise and they both lit up.

"We understand perfectly," said Buonarroti, breaking the silence, "that this won't stop the invasion of Moldovan workers. Things are good here, they're bad in Moldova, that's all there is to it. They'll keep coming here forever. Illegally. But if we don't turn down their visa requests, the entire country will storm Italy's walls!"

"Terrible," shuddered the colleague. "Really terrible."

"This way, at least, they leave the old folks, the children, and the unenterprising ones at home," explained the consul. "And they're obliged to send them money to somehow scrape by in the homeland."

"Those aren't our problems," remarked the consul's colleague drily.

"You're right. And so, our charge is to not grant anybody a visa. Nobody. If you grant a visa to just one person, you'll get overloaded with applications. I denied visas to a Moldovan water polo team traveling to a tournament in Milan. They were real water poloists, I know it. We wouldn't let a group of Moldovan Members of Parliament into Italy. We refused a group of journalists. Once we wouldn't let in an entire symphony orchestra that had been invited to Rome by Signor Berlusconi himself!"

"That's strict."

"What else can we do? I assure you, let the abovementioned into Italy, even if their visas aren't fraudulent, they're going to stay here no matter what."

"Honestly?"

"Yes. By the way, I'll let you in on a secret. But not a word to anybody. Do you know why the protocol desk back in Italy won't organize a meeting between Berlusconi and President Voronin of Moldova? Do you know why the meetings that had been planned in Italy were postponed for an undetermined date?"

"You're not saying …?"

"I am, I am, my friend. We have one hundred percent accurate information that the entire presidential delegation of Moldova, with the president himself at the helm, are planning to leave their hotel in Rome at night and spread out across Italy to set themselves up with work. One as a road paver, one as a shepherd on a farm, another as a maid …"

"My God!"

"That's nothing. Think about this: President Voronin himself collected four thousand euros from everybody in the delegation. That's the price human traffickers usually charge for the trip and a job once they arrive in Italy. The president himself!"

"Oh, my God," repeated his colleague, dumbstruck. "My God …"

"That's nothing, either. Because they even took four thousand euros from President Voronin himself!"

"That can't be!"

"That's not the whole of it. He paid four thousand euros so that, once he lands in Italy, he can sweat it out in a pizzeria as an assistant cook."

"Unbelievable … "

Buonarroti looked at his college with glee. He liked to surprise people. He nodded his head one more time, put out his cigarette and began passing his files to his successor. Buonarroti himself had been promoted. The post of Ambassador to Albania awaited him.

"Tell me, you don't come from *that* family, do you?" The new consul, his face reddening, had waited until dark to ask.

"The sculptor?" laughed the now former consul. "No,

indeed. Now matter how I searched for a family connection, I never found one. It's all because my old man was a big fan of a certain chap from Florence."

"I see," said his colleague.

"You're disappointed," smiled the former consul.

"Not at all, said his successor with surprise. "Why would I be?"

"You're disappointed," insisted Buonarroti. "I can tell. Everybody is disappointed when they find out. Everybody thinks a man who's called Michelangelo Buonarroti can't *not* be a descendant of the other man they called Michelangelo Buonarroti."

"Astute as always," admitted the new consul. "Forgive me."

Buonarroti smiled, stood up, walked over to the window. Above his right shoulder Bucharest's glittering, darkening central square was staring the new consul in the face.

"Plus, I've never done any sculpture work." Buonarroti sighed in the direction of the square below. "And I draw poorly."

The consul was very uncomfortable. "I apologize for bringi—"

"Nonsense," said Buonarroti. He waved his hand and turned around to face his colleague. "Let's get back to our Moldovans. Do you know that since they're all living in Italy illegally, they're completely terrified to leave the country."

"Because at the border they'll put them on the black list, and they'll never have a chance at Italy again," confirmed the consul.

"Absolutely right," nodded Buonarroti. "The only thing left is for them to send money home, write letters and make the occasional phone call. That's why, if you can imagine it, there are rumors going around Moldova that Italy doesn't exist."

"How ridiculous." The consul shrugged his shoulders, taking a seat in the chair against the wall. "Do you mind if I have a seat?"

"Please, not at all, especially since you already have. Plus, it's your chair now, anyway ... They're sure that the Italians in Italy have never heard of Moldovan workers. And as for this supposed country where two hundred thousand Moldovans vanish into thin air ... They think it's a myth, the invention of a gang of international swindlers who kidnap people. Or they think it's a fantasy. A mass hallucination."

"Then why do they come?"

Buonarroti shrugged his shoulders.

"Because things are in such a bad way in their homeland, they're ready to flee into a black hole in space, to a concentration camp, to the Sargasso Sea of international criminal brigands."

"Between the devil and the deep blue sea," said the new consul, demonstrating his knowledge of international idioms.

Buonarroti nodded and thrust the window all the way open. A restless Bucharest wind whisked through the room like a gypsy thief. The former consul stood a few moments more by the window, then parted ways with his replacement and headed home. Potato chip, nut and ice cream wrappers swirled around the gates of the consulate. "The kids from the local schools have been cutting class and coming here," thought the former consul. Kicking one of the wrappers, Buonarroti glumly recalled his childhood and the constant teasing he received from his classmates. His father and that stupid name – damn them both!

"A normal person wouldn't name his son Leonardo da Vinci, would he?" he muttered. He'd been having the same argument for forty years. Of course, his father had thought otherwise.

When Buonarroti arrived home, he glanced around the room where everything was already packed and peeked inside the hiding place his cleaning lady didn't know about. After extracting one hundred and twenty thousand euros, he hid the money in his pocket and laughed.

On the last day of work the former consul had sold a visa stamped "APPROVED" to a Moldovan curling team. Everything was in order. A secret investigation showed they were real athletes, absolutely set on participating in the competition in Italy and then continuing on to Beijing for another competition. Buonarroti wasn't a man who was usually for sale, and his conscience was tormenting him. But he had no other way out. In the last few years Buonarroti had lost a lot of dough on gambling. He needed the money in order to forever solve his one big problem: his name. But *changing* his name would have been a shameful escape, so he'd found the single means to overcome the malicious intent and mockery of his father.

Michelangelo Buonarroti was going to study to become a master sculptor.

13

Vasily Lungu had been fascinated by machines since childhood. Everything made by the hands of man brought him to sheer ecstasy – from the smallest plastic rabbit who banged a drum with his forepaws while standing on the back of a turtle, as a song drifted out of his head and his eyes sparkled, to the complicated structure of the Chisinau TV tower. This surprised his parents all the more since Vasya, like the past twenty generations of his ancestors, was a country boy to the core.

"Us Lungus – we don't know anything but the land," said Vasily's perplexed father, shrugging his shoulders. "And here my little whippersnapper only gives a hoot about machines ..."

From the age of five, Vasily's hands lost the smell of the earth peculiar to people who wake up before the cock crows. He was covered in machine grease. Gradually the boy's hands lost their sensitivity due to the various scratches and scars and injuries they sustained out of Vasily's carelessness with his tools. At ten years old, after spending the entire summer bent over in the tobacco fields, Vasily took the money he saved and bought a set of files, a soldering iron, a few vices and a circular saw. For this his father gave him a minor beating, but after Vasily fixed the television, his father stopped hounding his son for his strange obsession. And when official propaganda began extolling machines, it really wouldn't do to be ashamed of a son for the very activity the Soviet powers wished on all young people. Although sometimes, it's true, Vasya took his love for machines to the extreme.

"Listen up, old man." The chairman waved Vasily's father over for a serious conversation behind the house. "I have a feeling your son's making trouble."

"What's he done?" said the father, surprised. "Besides his gears and gadgets, what else can he think up? And even so, they're just gadgets ..."

"Follow me and you'll see," the chairman said. His voice was sinister and grim. Vasily's father suddenly felt especially uncomfortable and lonely in the dusty yard.

Sneaking up on the barn where Vasily did all his technical tinkering, the men cautiously opened the door a crack and peeked inside. Vasya wasn't home, he was working in the fields, so there was nothing to be afraid of. But all the same, it was scary. What if there was some devil's contraption in the barn?

And that's basically what they found. The chairman and Vasily's father looked at the strange construction in silent horror. Its shape was reminiscent of three bookcases stacked one on top of the other. Its function was unclear. The chairman managed to whisper that it reminded him of a giant ship with an abundance of sails. The only thing that came to the father's mind was his own exile to Siberia. A baby, he'd barely survived there with his kulak parents. The peasant didn't recall this out loud, however, as the current chairman was the one who'd sent them there. Why remind a good man of a bad deed?

"I wonder what it is," he said instead. "Up there, on top of the veneer, with those rods – that can't be rigging, can it?"

"Oh, that's rigging, alright, with rods, on top of the veneer," the chairman sneered venomously. "But unless we know the main thing, what's the use?"

"The what?" asked the father, frightened, and his heart squeezed up because he loved his son and because after Siberia his heart was weak, and his eyes prone to tears. "What don't the both of us know?"

The chairman frowned and clenched his teeth. "We don't know the *purpose* of this criminal apparatus your son constructed."

"Listen here, Koval," said Vasily's father, growing brave out of cowardice. "Don't you poke your nose around here, looking for my son. Far's I know, the Twentieth Congress is over. We exposed all you Stalinists for what you were. And I won't let you send my son to suffer in the North, like you sent me and mine. Understand?"

"Come on," said the chairman, genuinely offended. "Look, we'll send him somewhere and he'll be reeducated."

The father had tears in his eyes, remembering his years as a young boy in Siberia.

"I'll reeducate you with a pitchfork through your ribs," he said. And he promptly pinned the chairman against the wall of the barn with the farm instrument. The men stared at each other for a few minutes while the brightly colored village chickens raced by their feet like fleas. Vasily's father's eyes grew white, and he pressed the pitchfork harder. He himself nearly died of fear. After all, his entire life he'd been not a man, but a broken down old rag – though he wouldn't admit it to anyone. He was afraid of everything, and he often cried at night when he remembered his father: how his old man would return to that northern settlement with hands bloodstained from the slave labor, biting his lip as Mother rubbed ointment into the wounds ... how his mother used to collect pinecones at night, so nobody would see, and peel them, then pound the seeds and add them to the bread ... how the supplies ran out in January of the long Siberian winter and his brother, his beloved brother, five-year-old Greisha, who had swollen up from hunger, his stomach bloated, at death's door, kept asking Mama for something to eat. And one day he stopped asking ...

Vasily's father's eyes filled with tears as he remembered his parents, dead not long after returning from exile. He threw nearly all his weight onto the pitchfork. The chairman was saved by the secret file he'd tucked beneath his shirt.

Koval's shock turned to fear and he tried to relieve the tension.

"Well, maybe he's not a damaging element, your sonny boy," he appeased with a mutter. "Maybe he ended up, say, in a Trotskyite circle by mistake, and then knocked this together."

"And what *is* this?" asked the boy's father, crying again. "Maybe it's nothing to worry about!"

"Just look closely," said the chairman again, bravely. "How can such a thing not be dangerous, suspicious and seditious?!?"

Vasily's father sighed, let go of the pitchfork and sat down on his haunches. He stared intently at his son's mishmash. What was there to say? It did look dangerous, suspicious and seditious. And that could mean only one thing. They'd lock up his son. The father's heart tensed up and froze forever. From then on, he developed a little stutter and his lower lips would tremble from time to time. The chairman watched with satisfaction as his fellow villager suffered, and regretted not having the chance to take a picture of the scene to hang on the wall of shame at the Larga town office. For in the depths of his heart a Stalinist he remained, Twentieth Congress be damned.

"Hey, what are you doing here?" Vasily froze at the threshold of the barn. "Papa? Comrade Chairm ..."

He hadn't finished speaking when his father threw himself at his feet, sobbing.

"Oh, Vasya, Vasenka, tell me, what have you gotten yourself into?" he begged. "What's this devil's machine you've got here? Confess! We're going together to the regional offices, we're turning ourselves in. When you turn yourself in you don't suffer as much. Oh, flesh of my flesh, what have you done?"

"Let him write a confession," suggested the chairman, businesslike. He'd settled back on his haunches. "I've got a piece of paper and a pen. Just make sure to specify at the bottom that it was me, Chairman Koval, who with his vigilance helped expose these intrigues."

"He'll specify, he'll specify," sobbed Vasily's father, writing. "He'll specify everything, just don't make him suffer, let him alone, you cretins. My only son!"

The chairman was already scribbling. " 'Cretins' is going into the report, as well!" He stuck out his tongue.

At first Vasily didn't understand a thing. When he realized what was going on, he broke out in laughter. He threw open the barn window and the chickens flew up, up and away, feathers swirling, and the fresh air flew in, and Vasily laughed so long and so contagiously that his father's eyes leaked as if somebody had poked them out. And the father understood that the times had changed, and nobody was going to execute his only son, and that the boy—a member of the Youth Komsomol and an A student in physics, chemistry and mathematics, and, well, in literature there was room for improvement—the boy hadn't done anything wrong. And Chairman Koval also understood it, and with sadness he tore up the confession and the report he'd already filled out. Vasya had laughed himself out and walked up to the strange apparatus that engendered so much suspicion in the vigilant chairman.

"Now, you son of a bitch, I want you to drag the first Soviet replica of the first Wright Brothers plane to the village square."

14

"Comrades! In front of us we have the first Soviet replica of the first Wright Brothers plane – which makes it the first replica of the first plane in the world!"

Seventeen year-old Vasily began his lecture. He was handsome, with a resemblance to the latest fashionable movie star.

The crowd was respectfully silent, watching as Vasily slowly drew circles around the apparatus—which didn't look like an airplane at all—with his pointer. Nobody protested, since thanks to the lecture they'd been let off work in the orchards and the fields. Not far from the villagers, the chairman of the regional VSCAAF, the Volunteer Society for Cooperation with the Army, Aviation and Fleet, paced up and down, happy that in a village in his jurisdiction there was to be found a natural-born mechanic.

"And what, comrades, exactly is this Wright Brothers plane?" asked Vasily. Then he added maliciously, "A plane that a few of our comrades took for a strange and suspicious mishmash?"

"Vasenka," whispered Koval, using an endearing nickname for the boy. "Sweet boy …"

Vasya smiled gloatingly and continued his lecture. He'd decided the following with the chairman: Vasily wouldn't say anything about Koval's subversive idea to call the first Soviet replica of the Wright Brothers plane a suspicious mishmash; in return, Koval would have to fly as the copilot.

"Don't worry, scumbag," Vasily growled as they dragged

the plane to the village council. "The machine runs like clockwork, I've already tested it. We'll fly low, about two hundred meters off the ground. And not for too long, either. About three miles. Then we'll turn around."

"Vasya, I'm afraid of heights," whimpered the chairman. "Don't …"

"As you well should be, scumbag." Vasya, who never used bad language, nodded his head. "But I'll be flying with you. So you're not going to die."

"Vasya, I'm afraid of hei …"

"I know. That's why you're going to fly. And you're going to cry, you animal – you'll cry all my family's tears, and the tears of my murdered Uncle Greisha."

"Vasya, you're speaking like an anti-Soviet," said Koval, wiping his tears.

"No," Vasily smiled. "You're the anti-Soviet, because you nearly suspected the first Soviet replica of the Wright Brothers plane of being a suspicious mishmash! And I made it in secret, to bring joy to the Moldovan Communist Party and its Secretary, Comrade Bodiul. And to the leadership of the entire USSR and to Comrade Brezhnev. And you, you scumbag, you wanted to mess with the happiness of Comrade Brezhnev and Comrade Bodiul. So what does that make you now?

"An anti-Soviet," whispered the defeated Koval. "Oh, people – forgive me."

They dragged the plane outside and Koval set off for the office, to tell the regional bosses about the seventeen-year-old self-taught Vasily Lungu, who joined the VSCAAF and made the first Soviet replica of the Wright Brothers plane all in order to make the party, Comrade Bodiul and Comrade Brezhnev proud. The bosses in Chisinau reported back their decision to send the plane on a tour of Moldova, to give the people a jolt and infect the youth with a yearning skywards. And they decided the first lecture would be delivered in Larga, in the hometown of the seventeen-year-old self-taught Vasily Lungu, who joined the VSCAAF and made the first Soviet replica of the Wright Brothers plane, all in order to make the party, Comrade Bodiul and Comrade Brezhnev proud.

The chairman thought about the impending flight and let out a cry. But in his heart he understood that going for a spin in an airplane was peanuts compared to what he had done to Vasily's family. He cried anyway. It seemed like the thing to do. Meanwhile, Vasily kept talking and the crowd was transfixed. Nobody expected such a silver tongue from a boy from Larga!

"Actually, Comrades, I lied to you," said Vasya, sadly. "I lied to my fellow villagers, I lied to the comrades from the region and to my friends from the Komsomol organization."

"Aha!" The people said in surprise. "Oho!"

Vasya gave a wide grin and shook an unruly lock of his ink-black hair.

"I told you there was an airplane in front of you. But I lied. This is no plane."

"Aha," said the audience, surprised and scared.

"Oho," Chairman Koval's heart skipped a happy beat and he reached into his pocket for the scraps of paper with the report and confession.

"In front of you, Comrades," said Vasily, aiming his pointer, "is not exactly an airplane; it's actually a biplane glider – just a bit bigger and more durable."

Cries of "Oho!" rang out happily from the crowd.

"Aha," exclaimed Koval, bitterly. "Aha …"

"And a twelve horsepower gasoline engine weighing over two hundred and twenty pounds is sitting on the rear wing," said Vasya, under the proud gaze of his father. "Next to that, you can see the pilot's seat and the steering rudders. Do you know how much steam the motor picks up?"

"More than our tractors?" the newly-minted mechanics shouted boisterously. "Impossible!"

"Possible," Vasily answered boisterously. "The motor can reach fifteen hundred rpms and with the help of a train drive it turns two pusher propellers three meters wide, laid out symmetrically in back of the wings."

"Well, I'll be!" said the surprised mechanics.

"That's right!" laughed Vasily. "And now, Comrades, in order to demonstrate the effectiveness of this machine, how easy a time she has up in the air, how pretty she looks, we're going to take an experimental flight."

"Hurrah!" rejoiced the young people. "Choose me, Vasily! Choose me!"

"No, Comrades, I've already promised the first flight to our chairman, Secretary Koval," said Vasily, chewing his lip sympathetically. "Our joint flight will be a symbol of the link between the Komsomol youths and the tried-and-true party elders. It is only to Comrade Koval that I can offer the copilot seat on this, the first Soviet replica of the Wright Brothers plane, built in order to bring joy to the party and Comrade Badiul and Comrade Brezhnev ..."

"Hurrah!" answered the young folks, enviously.

The crowd triumphantly lifted Koval and Vasily in the air. From that alone the chairman felt sick. Finally, the crowd put them back on their feet and Vasya helped the chairman put on his silly helmet and climb onto the wing, and then into the cockpit. Vasily, too, got in. A group of young Largans took hold of a cable and dragged the glider to give it speed, after which the machine caught an airstream and took off. Shaky, unsure of itself – but it took off. From down below, the plane looked so exhilarating that Vasily's father teared up again. Even Chairman Koval was so taken by the beautiful view opening up as they climbed heavenward that he forgot his fear.

"What do you think, bloodsucker?" Vasily turned toward him and laughed. "Afraid yet?"

"No," smiled Koval, groping in his pocket for the report. "No, I'm not afraid anymore. It's so beautiful!"

"Tell me, what was it like to eat people alive, eh?" Vasily asked suddenly. The question was so serious and full of thought that the chairman, not expecting such pep from a seventeen-year-old kid, went cold.

"What you're feeling's not fear," said Vasya, as if he were reading Koval's mind. "It's the ascending altitude."

"Ah!" shouted the chairman. He was happy and relieved. "For a minute there I ... Listen, Vasya, you have to understand, the times were different. Sure, we cracked some eggs. But we put the country on its feet."

"Atop the bones of my uncle, who died from hunger as a baby in Siberia?" asked Vasily, once again proving tougher than his years.

"You know, it ..." Koval was completely flustered. "Well ..."

"Enough," shouted Vasily, "the hell with you, you're all bastards. You know, I pulled a fast one on you, too."

"What was that?" shouted the chairman happily, since they could barely hear each other on account of the wind.

The plane circled above the rapids of the Dniester. In the north of Moldova, the Dniester looks wild when glimpsed from the sky, and the white limestone hills sparkle at the river's edge like the bones of some strange animal who lived in the sea that was once here billions of years ago ...

"I told you it was the first Soviet replica of the first Wright Brothers plane," shouted Vasily at the top of his lungs. "But in the first Wright Brothers plane, there was no seat for a copilot. Me and you, chairman, we're flying in the first Soviet replica of the *second* Wright Brothers plane!"

"Peanuts!" said Koval, bobbing his head. "So what, so what. The main thing is —it's a replica! The party's happy! That's the main thing!"

"Oh yeah," said Vasily, as the plane climbed higher and higher on the airstreams. "There's one more thing I lied to you about."

"Again?" said Koval, then added: "Maybe we've gone high enough?"

"The earth is round," laughed Vasily. "Everything's relative. Maybe we're falling."

"What do you mean?" asked Koval.

"Eh, don't worry about it." Vasya waved his hand, the plane swerved, and the chairman's heart tore a hole through his shirt. "So you want to know what I lied about?"

"Spit it out already," said Koval, "and let's start our descent."

"The second Wright Brothers plane didn't have a bomb hatch. Ours, the Soviet replica of the second Wright Brothers plane, does. And what does that mean? It means it's not a replica of the second Wright Brothers plane, either!"

"Sure, sure," said the chairman, fawning cheerfully. He was far removed from aviation and none of this meant anything to him. "Sure, sure. So, when are we going to descend, huh?!"

"You?" said Vasily, turning toward him. His face lit up. "Before you can say, 'Now!'"

Vasily pulled the lever for the hatch. Spinning slowly, like a scuba diver backing into the water, Koval realized he was falling. At first he was frightened, and then he rejoiced at the unforgettable feeling of flight. Then he was distressed again because, after all, he *was* flying toward his death. And beyond that border, the old Bolshevik Comrade Koval knew, there was nothing, nothing at all to speak of.

And in fact, he was right. There *was* nothing. Neither big agriculture, nor Communist Party; no Soviet replica of the first, second or third Wright Brothers plane; no goddamn Greisha Lungu—who used to visit the chairman in his dreams from time to time—swollen from hunger, dead in Siberia; there were no sobbing men, no laughing women, no happy young lads with movie star looks. Terrifying to think of it – no movie stars, either! And no svelte Soviet pop singers and not even the Secretary of the Moldovan Communist Party, Comrade Bodiul – even he didn't exist down below, in the land after death, where there were no vineyards, no sun, no shame, no confessions. The single, solitary thing that exists down there is this: Nothing.

But the chairman could no longer confirm nor deny. And having ceased to be—*Finito!*—he couldn't be sure whether he'd ceased to be. *Finito!*

The investigation revealed that Koval, drunk on the fresh high-altitude air and the beautiful view, acted recklessly and was responsible for his own fall. Vasya barely managed to land the plane, which suffered irreparable damage, and so it was impossible to carry out a follow-up flight investigation. They buried the chairman on the highest hill in the village. On his gravestone they placed a monument, a five-pointed marble slab with a plane carved on it, and stars suspended above. In the newspaper *Independent Moldova*, there was a lofty obituary with the title, "He gave his life to the earth, his death – to the sky!"

The national VSCAAF held a grand competition the year after Koval's death, which became, as the press so aptly remarked, a fine tradition. Moldovan pioneer scouts composed songs and poems about the simple village toiler who, for sixty years, worked to feed the Soviet Union, gaining bloody calluses on his hand, and who dreamed of the heavens in his heart. When he was already at retirement age—although he thought it corrupt to allow himself to take the government's money for a pension—he flew in the sky with a young Komsomol member. Their plane lost control and the Komsomol member was inexperienced. Comrade Koval told him, "Be calm, son, I'll save you," and jumped out of the plane to maintain equilibrium. Koval went down, and the Komsomol member landed the plane in tears.

Of course, there was also a school named in the chairman's honor. And in the village council they hung a marble plaque with his portrait. But that all happened later. Right after the tragedy, maybe a month later, Komsomol member Lungu was issued an honorary Komsomol trip to somewhere out of harm's way.

"Vasily, we're sending you to tractor school," the new chairman grandly announced to the young man. "At least when you fall out of a tractor, you won't die!"

15

As he was remembering this, Vasily Lungu, with his friend, Serafim Botezatu, gulped down a few jugs of wine.

"Admit it," said Serafim, smiling. "You ejected the chairman from the airplane on purpose."

"No!," said Vasya, and crossed himself. "Cross my heart. Orthodox style, with the Life-Giving Cross."

"What difference does it make, your Life-Giving Cross?" said Serafim. "Anyway, you don't believe in God."

"I've flown through heaven," Vasily laughed. "It was empty."

"Tfu." Serafim said. Then he spit, more out of form than conviction. "So tell me, you want to go back again? Up there?"

"No," lied Vasily. "What business have I got in the skies? Back then, I admit, the only reason I even got started with the whole thing was thanks to the chairman."

"Aren't you afraid?"

"We've had a new order here for twenty years, Serafim! These days they'd probably give me a letter of commendation for killing a Bolshevik!"

"They won't give you anything—"

"Exactly …"

"Here."

"Meaning? What are you trying to say?" Lungu asked.

"I'm trying to say, a man with hands like yours has got no business staying in Moldova," Serafim blurted out.

"Akh," said Vasily and waved his hand. "You're on

about that again. About your stinking Italy …"

"Not stinking at all," argued Serafim. "Blessed, beautiful and surprising. Come on. Have you seen our river crossing at the Dniester? It's dirty, it's skimpy. It's basically just a name, not even a bridge. But in Venice, you know, there's an entire city built on piles. It's a city in the sea. And everywhere – bridges, bridges, bridges. It's clean, it's neat. Out-of-this-world beauty. The salaries are enormous. Tell me, would you want to become a gondolier?"

"What, so I can pull oars all day and cover my hands in calluses? I can get calluses here if I want them." Vasily shrugged his shoulders.

"Moron," Serafim upbraided him. "They've been using motorboats for a long time."

"Motorboats?" asked Vasily, dreamily. Then he shook his head. "No. It's not for me."

"What's more," pressed Serafim, while the iron was still hot, "there are factories there. Fiat. Everything's mechanized, everything's covered in machine grease. The steel thunders, grumbles … Ekh!"

"Machine grease," said Vasya …

"I could set you up there," Serafim said casually. "A guy I know from the village of Varzaresti has been in Italy five years now. He called me a little while ago. He can't help me get to Italy, he says, but once I'm there, he'll find me a job. And you, too, and whoever else you come with.

"At Fiat?"

"At Fiat."

The men were silent a while. Vasily ponderously spun a bicycle chain in his hands. What he would use it for, he wasn't sure yet, but he'd been hoping to find a solution to this problem all evening. Serafim had distracted him from his task. Vasily was mad at his friend, but his anger dissipated.

"And how are we supposed to get there?" he asked Serafim glumly. "Borrow money again? Nobody'd give it to us."

"We don't need money."

"Oh yeah? How then? By God's grace, or what? They don't let beggars cross borders."

"Who's talking border crossings? We'll bypass them."

"Oh yeah, how?" asked Vasily stubbornly.

"In an airplane." Serafim was calm; he knew that Vasily was softening. "In an airplane, my good man …"

"Plane tickets cost money!" Vasilly was vexed. He raised his voice. "I've been trying to explain that to you for two hours!"

Serafim took a sip of wine and rubbed his hands.

"We won't have to pay to get on this plane," he explained, satisfied. "We're going to take our own plane. And you're the one who's going to make it!"

Vasily, at a loss for words, gathered air into his lungs and held it. For a minute he sat motionless. Finally, he exhaled and, inhaling again, lifted a finger.

"We're going in an airplane that *I'm* going to make?"

"We're going in an airplane that *you're* going to make," confirmed Serafim.

"To Italy?"

"To Italy."

"To the Fiat factory?"

"To the Fiat factory."

Vasily was quiet. When he started talking again, he grew more and more animated.

"The model I built in my younger days won't work. That was a biplane, and it barely held its equilibrium. The first gust of wind would smash us back to the earth. We'll have to build a real solid airplane. Real solid."

"From what?" inquired Serafim, all business. "What material will we use?"

Vasily thought a moment. Then he said:

"We're going to steal my tractor."

16

Marian Lupu, Speaker of the Parliament of Moldova, with a look of outward intelligence quite unusual for a man in his position, straightened his back with pleasure and wiped the sweat from his brow.

"Marusya, bring me some of that yummy water," he boomed in a stentorian voice to his spouse. "I need a drink, and how!"

His wife snorted and went to the well for some water. Of course, there *was* running water in the modest three-storey house, which President Voronin had given to Lupu when he rose to his current position. There was water, too, in the four summer pavilions standing at the corners of the vast piece of land. Water for any taste. Carbonated mineral water, uncarbonated water, carbonated plain water, alkaline water, rainwater, meltwater, luxurious French Perrier and its modest Moldovan imitation, sweet water and water with juice, water with sugar and sherbet, and finally, *kvas* and beer. But Lupu demanded his wife bring him nothing but water from the well. He liked to watch her shapely back as she strained her muscles and turned the crank. He liked to stare at her as she nearly stooped to see if the bucket was nigh; he liked how she drew it out of the well and, splashing her bare feet, carried the clean well water to him.

But how could the speaker have known that the well was filled with tepid water, and that a specially-trained scuba diver was swimming inside, on duty around the clock? Catching sight of Lupu's bride above the surface of the

The Good Life Elsewhere

water, the scuba diver hefted onto the chain not the old rusty bucket the speaker was so fond of, but a clever imitation: a silver pail with gilding made to look like rust, tightly closed with a special lid. When the water reached the top, the lid fell off, all by itself. A special mechanized lift was attached to the crank and the statesman's wife only pretended to strain herself. And Lupu was the recipient of water specially filtered in a laboratory ...

Lupu knew none of this, and with pleasure his gaze followed his wife as she brought him the pail of water. Marusya wasn't her name, actually, but it was so resonant of ancient folk tales that he called her that anyway. What difference did it make to the head of the country's legislative body, when he wished to get back to a simpler life and become one with nature, in a bond à la ancient Rus. All the more, since this was an act of domestic protest by Lupu, in light of the—to put it delicately—worsening relations between Moldova and Russia.

"In light of worsening relations ... In light of this, in light of that ..." scoffed Lupu. "What's with this jibber-jabber? Why can't diplomats ever use normal, human language? Although, to be honest, is there such a thing as non-human language? I don't mean purely hypothetically. I mean concretely, of course, even somewhat empirically speaking—"

And at this point the speaker, a lover of high-flown verbal formulations, completely confused himself and bent down to get back to work. Marian Lupu was hoeing a potato patch. This too was part of his program of returning to the simpler life. And, curse though his wife did, she still sacrificed a few meters of earth from underneath her flowers to her husband's potatoes. Of course, it was the gardener who cared for the flowers, but she put so much heart into them, the poor thing, that the tongue just couldn't call them anything but her own. And with praiseworthy stubbornness, her husband watered his potato patch with his sweat. He took heart in the hard peasant's work, which stretched his every last muscle and in which the true son of Moldova, our speaker, found repose. At least, that's what the state press service reported about Lupu's weekends.

From time to time, when his wife stayed over in Chisinau, Lupu conducted raids in his potato patch. He never sprayed his plants to protect them from Colorado beetles; he preferred to collect the striped sons of bitches himself, by hand. His hands turned yellow like the poet Mayakovsky's jacket, about whose work Marian wrote his dissertation, and he would get a faraway look on his face. Collecting an entire jarful of beetles, Lupu would fall into a trance, so it seemed, and slowly make his way around the house, to the paved driveway. There, he would sit down on the curb. One by one he extracted the beetles and butchered them with a small hatchet. At first rarely, then more and more frequently, the speaker would chop off the beetle's head with one blow and watch from the sidelines as the headless, striped, barrel-like little thing— the beetle's body—scampered madly across the pavement for a few moments.

"Hey there, Iurie," he said in a mechanical voice to a huge beetle. "Iurie Rosca!"—this was the name of the leader of the nationalist opposition party—"How are you?" *Smack*! "Oh! What's happened to Mister Rosca's head? It flew bye-bye? And who do we have here? Mister Victor Stepaniuc himself, alive and in person ..." Stepaniuc was a member of parliament representing the Communist Party. *Smack*! "Opa, we missed our mark. The spine is sliced but the head's not chopped! All covered in booboos, but alive, like Marx's doctrine, ha ha ha!" *Smack*! "Oh, Marx! Hello. How are things with you? Opa! Oh no, for you even the axe is too good. We'll just use our foot again." *Smack*! "Oh, just look at that. Mister Serafim Urechean, alive and in person! Former communist, pan-Europeanist!" *Swish*! "There goes half the torso!" *Smack*! "Farewell, head. And you, sir, you must be President Smirnov, I presume." *Crack, crack*. Smirnov was the president of the breakaway republic of Transnistria. "Oh!! Such a meaty one ... so healthy ... President Voronin! Alive and in person! For you, it'll be a match under your belly!"

Toward dusk, Lupu would sadly toss aside his hatchet and wash his trembling hands in the silver basin beside the southern wall of the house. The metallic sliver of moon in the Moldovan night would come to a point and scratch the side of Lupu's face, and he'd come to. Then he'd scrub and scrub the yellow guts of the murdered beetles off the road and carefully rinse the jar. And toward morning—bright-eyed, happy, fresh-faced—he would return to Chisinau, where he'd live quietly for another year. Until his body would start to ache again, his lips would burn, his temples would blaze with heat, his heart would beat madly, and reason would tell him it was time to go back to the country house and start gathering those Colorado beetles ...

But that's all in the past – or the future. Right now, the Speaker of Parliament Marian Lupu has tilled his potato patch and is admiring his wife, who is carrying the sweet water in a rusty steel bucket. The water is tastiest from the well, the speaker knows. He waits until his wife approaches, carefully grabs the bucket from her hands and hoists it up to his head. He doesn't like drinking from a cup. It feels ungenerous. And before he is able to swallow, he looks up at the sky and plops right down on the patch of land, as if afraid of something, yet without spilling a single drop of water. His wife looks at him with surprise and heads home to summon the doctor from the speaker's security detail. The doctor will be the one who later on spreads various rumors for which the authorities will dispatch him to the province of Kagul as a veterinary inspector. There, he will happily drink his life away. And from time to time he'll take to swearing that Lupu, before falling asleep, whispered the words: "A tractor! A tractor flew over my head ..."

17

THE GUTS OF THE TRACTOR HAD TO BE RIPPED OUT, VASILY explained. In its place, they installed the airplane motor from the first Soviet replica of the Wright Brothers plane—who knew which Wright Brothers plane, exactly?—which Lungu had saved all these twenty-five years of his willed exile from aviation, when he worked as a tractor mechanic. They installed the machinery, the wings, and even put in a small tank of combustible gas. They made no changes to the body of the tractor, which was made of light, thin sheets of metal. This way, they would "completely disorient the anti-aircraft defenses of the countries lying en route to the destination," Vasily explained.

"And now what?" yelled Serafim, slapping Vasily on the back. "What's next? We don't have playing cards, or anything!"

"We're approaching Chisinau," Vasily said, manipulating the controls. "We'll discretely circle over the airport, fall in with a plane going to Bucharest, and fly on its tail. Then we'll repeat the tactic and fly to Budapest. And then, on to Slovenia. From there it's only a stone's throw from Italy."

"Genius!" roared Serafim and embraced the embarrassed Vasya. "Goddamn genius!"

"Yeah, but you know, it's a shame we didn't think of this before," Vasily said again. "My wife wouldn't have had to go hang herself ... "

He put the aircraft on autopilot and the friends drank a glass of wine in honor of poor Maria's soul. Then they drank a glass in honor of their happy takeoff and a happy landing. They ate a few snacks and drank again, this time just because. Then Vasily turned back around in his pilot's seat and steered the craft into the clouds.

"What are you doing that for?" said Serafim. The pressure was messing with his eardrums, and he was confused. "It's all damp here, like in a water-filled basement."

"When we're above cities we'll always go into the clouds," Vasily explained. "This way we don't call any extra attention to ourselves."

"Smart thinking," agreed Serafim. "I'm sorry I doubted you."

"Let's drink to Italy!" Vasily suggested. "To Italy, home of the Fiat!"

"And to Italy, home to Venice and its bridges!"

"To our Italy, the only one, different and inimitable for each person, the way only a true lover can be!"

"To Italy! *Vivat Italia!*"

The heavenly tractor, rattling along, plowed its propeller unhurriedly through the fog and the friends dozed off.

18

Vladimir Voronin, President of Moldova, shifted his weight from left foot to right foot and nostalgia set in. It had been three hours since he was supposed to have kicked his shoes off and been highstepping through the grass near the Dniester River. Fishing, inhaling the smoke of a bonfire and drinking cognac strong as righteous tears. Instead, he was standing on a podium in a suit that choked him, his feet in shabby socks squeezed into narrow shoes. And it looked like he'd be standing there for a while.

"You couldn't find me any other shoes?" the president asked the office manager who was dressing him for the meeting. "I look like a trader from Azerbaijan at the outdoor market!"

"That's who we bought them from!" the office manager stupidly concurred. "They say, these are the socks of President Aliyev of Azerbaijan himself!"

"Aliyev," the president mocked, stuffing his feet into the shoes. "And you believed them, you numbskull!"

And he set off for the meeting regarding the adoption of the Moldova – European Union plan, which had zero meaning but was being publicized to distract the people from their poverty.

"Keep harping on about how Europe's close to accepting you," the American ambassador to Moldova suggested coldly to the president, when the latter came to ask for a loan. "They'll grab onto that like a rabbit after a carrot. But I'm sorry. I can't give you any money."

Speaker Lupu was the one who should have been speaking.

He was younger and more eloquent, but, the president was informed, something had happened to the speaker. He'd gotten overheated while working in his garden and suffered a heat stroke. He mumbled some nonsense about flying tractors or floating trucks, nobody could make any damn sense of it. The president sighed and began reading:

"The expansion of the European Union, initiated on May 1, 2004, signifies an historic change to the EU in political, geographical and economic directions, strengthening the future political and economic partnership between Moldova and the European Union, nnn, nnnnn, nnnnnnzzzzzzzzzzz ... "

"Mister President, Mister President, you're snoring," whispered the head of the Foreign Ministry, tugging at his neighbor's sleeve.

"Ah, mmmh. Excuse me." Voronin shook his head and started reading again to the three thousand people gathered on the square.

"This presents an opportunity for advancement consistent with harmonization, raising the level of economic integration and the deepening of political cooperation. It is incumbent upon the European Union and Moldova to take advantage of the proposed opportunities for the strengthening of mutual relations and the promotion of stability, safety and prosperity. Our unique and shared characteristics, and our current partnership will serve as the basis for this development, and its enactment will initiate future growth in the strategic partnership between nnn, nnnnn, nnnnnnzzzzzzzzzzz ... "

This time his neighbor didn't even have to intercede, for the President woke himself up with his own snoring. And, as always when he was half-asleep, he was pissed. To hell with them all!

"And now, to tell you about the immediate future of Moldova in Europe, is our Minister of Foreign Affairs," he exclaimed. "I'm sorry for the microphone malfunction.

Clearly, our technicians, too, want to be in Europe so badly they've all set off without waiting for the end of their president's speech!"

The crowd laughed and the president walked toward the steps, behind the backs of the ambassadors, ministers and advisors who weren't leaving. "Let them stand there," the president decided, "I'm going fishing in the Dniester."

Voronin looked bitterly at the backsides of the milieu. "To hell with them. Let them get wet," he said tersely.

But after taking two steps, he thought about the political opposition and sighed. Once again, they'd blame him and the ruling party for all of Moldova's troubles. The headlines flashed before his eyes: "Communists Say They Want Europe, but Soak European Representatives in the Rain," or "President Voronin Subjects the Representatives of European Integration to a Humiliating Sojourn in the Rain." And, sighing yet again, he decided to issue an order to disperse the clouds. He sighed a third time, thinking about the reaction from the Russian Ambassador. The President could almost hear the notes ring out:

"The government of Moldova's alliance with supporters of so-called European values is completely incomprehensible. In their desire to oblige their allies, the Moldovans even went so far as to inflict violence upon nature, chasing clouds away in an easterly direction (incidentally, of course), stopping at nothing ... Meanwhile, the government of Moldova has lost sight of the fact that ... Sincere apologies ... Absolutely incomprehensible, provoking consternation on the part of the Russian Federation ... "

And what about the reactions of all the autonomous, breakaway regions? What would they say? And how about the Organization for Security and Cooperation in Europe? The only side that wouldn't sling mud would be the newspaper *The Communist*, and even there they'd whisper in the corner that—*Have you heard?*—the president has strayed from party ideals ... And where are they, these ideals? Ah, sons of bitches, all of them!

Biting his lips, Voronin understood he had to choose. Reflecting for a minute, he recalled that the Russian Ambassador Rybov had already *not* been giving him loans for a year. And in general, the man was condescending and unpleasant. The American ambassador, meanwhile, was quite friendly, though he also wasn't loaning any money. But in contrast to the Russian ambassador, the American had *never* been in the habit ...

"Oh, kiss my ass, all of them," Voronin said to the mayor. "Shoot the clouds a few times to disperse them, but no more. I don't want anybody to be able to raise a stink. Is that clear?"

The mayor leaped into action and the president, settling into the seat in his Volvo, took off his shoes and socks and began wiggling his numbed toes with great pleasure. He thought about how nice it would be to change the government in Chisinau. A very obsequious chap, that mayor. Not like his predecessor, who Voronin had had to fire for obstinacy. Change the bureaucrats and then it would be smooth sailing for the president, a man whom even seedy Italy had barred from entering its territory for three years running. "Oh, they can all kiss my ass!" Voronin repeated to himself.

Toward noon, the cloud the tractor had been sailing in was pierced by a bullet. Serafim and Vasily were saved thanks only to the ejection device, and touched ground right in the forest surrounding Chisinau.

"Well, at least we tried," said Serafim. He wiped the blood off his beat-up face.

And thus, a meeting about European cooperation be-

came an insurmountable obstacle on the path of two Moldovans on their way into Europe.

19

THE OLD PEASANT TOOK A SEAT ON THE DOORSTEP OF HIS house and groaned.

"Well, sonny boy, they say whoever goes to Italy never comes back! But the people who've made it – they don't complain, just like a bunch of daisy pushers. Italy, it turns out, is just like heaven! And there's no road back for whoever makes it up there."

The young man was entranced; he sat on his haunches beside the old peasant and wrote down the man's words in a lined notebook. On the notebook's cover, a made-up Britney Spears stretched open her mouth in a silent scream. The elderly peasant was clearly confused, and Octavian Gonts, a student in the Philological Department at Moldova State University, was ashamed of the young, debauched singer who was exposing herself on the cover of his school notebook. But there was nothing to be done, he hadn't been able to find any others at the railroad station twenty miles from Larga. And, as usual, it slipped his mind to take paper and a pen with him from Chisinau.

The dean of the university, a famous Moldovan poet, had offered words of encouragement to Octavian and three other students:

"You're setting off for the far-flung corners of Moldova, where the barbarian hand of Moscow never touched our people's difficult and complex soul. There, you'll find the Moldova of Stefan the Great. You'll talk with people who remember their roots and know where they came from and why. Be vigilant, and work tirelessly."

And the mini-expedition of folklorists from the Philological Department set off on their journey. They'd been in Larga a week now. The trip, intended to last only a few days, had been extended and the students were excited. The dean had proved right: they'd never before gathered such an amount of folklore material in one population point in Moldova. What was especially gratifying to the young researchers was that in Larga, new myths were being intertwined with old legends.

"For example, just listen to the stories about Italy!" Octavian exclaimed enthusiastically, sitting around the campfire at dinner. "The old superstitions about heaven and St. Peter from the times of the Turkish occupation have been fancifully woven together with notions of the promised land these poor plow-pushers have today."

Elena Syrbu interrupted Octavian. "I'm hearing echoes of the eschatological drama of the beginning of our era, the drama at the birth of Christianity." She was a standout and the favorite student in the course. "And such thrilling observ—"

"And this village," said the student Lipan, looking dreamily up at the sky, "has given birth so many parables, philosophical ideas, so many, shall we say, delineations."

The young people were ecstatic. Having awakened early in the morning, they dispersed throughout Larga, each one with an enormous notebook and several pens, to harvest the oral vineyards of the peasants, to reap the fragrant fields of their fantasies, to humbly water the seedlings of the ambitious residents, seedlings which were breaking their way through a thick stratum of mistrust. Now there was something to really be proud of! The entire folklore expedition had taken an interest in these stories.

There was yet another reason why Octavian wanted their expedition to last forever. He was hopelessly—and secretly (although the entire department and half the university knew about it)—in love with his fellow student, Elena Syrbu. Alas, the feelings weren't mutual. She was as unwelcoming toward him as the barren land near Balti, as prickly as the blackthorn in the gypsy fields near Soroca. She tormented him with her mockery like the summer sun burns the wastelands of Gagauzia. But she didn't spurn him completely. The attentions of Octavian, so full of hope, were flattering, after all.

"I'd marry a guy like that in a heartbeat," Elena's roommate in the dormitories told her excitedly. "He's handsome, passionate, a young genius!"

"But he's got no backbone," parried Elena. "If he encounters any insurmountable obstacles, he'll drink himself to ruin, like all geniuses."

"Then send him packing!"

The practical, pretty Elena objected: "What's the point of me driving him away if there's a chance he *won't* encounter any insurmountable obstacles and he'll become world famous? A man like that, I could marry."

"And what if you can't wait that long?"

"I'll take pleasure in the fact that the famous researcher Octavian, back when he was just a poor little thing, was hopelessly in love with me … "

Octavian understood everything but couldn't do anything about it. Elena had become a part of his life more permanently than a sarcoma tumor in a diseased man's lungs; deeper than a narcotic in the bloodstream; more tenaciously than a louse in one's hair. He couldn't evict her from his life without displacing himself, too. For the time being, though, his love of folklore was saving him.

Octavian watched as dusk danced and swirled passionately with the light from the campfire across Elena's face. "When we finish collecting the data, I'm going to begin work on a new theory."

"Oh really?" asked the pretty girl reluctantly, without looking away up the campfire. "What theory might that be?"

Octavian was full of fervor. "It seems that contemporary Italy takes the place of a general afterlife in the consciousness of the peasants," he started to say.

Elena, who was an outstanding linguist but a wanting historian, interrupted him.

"There's no such thing as a 'general afterlife.' There's a division between hell and heaven."

"But that's a tradition that came later," Octavian patiently explained to the girl he was secretly in love with. "What we've got here are early Hellenic traditions that *somehow* survived into the twenty-first century. You don't think that's surprising?"

"Why?"

"It would be like ... like finding the remains of a village from the Stone Age right in the middle of modern London! Can you imagine?"

"To be honest, not really."

"Alright, fine. At any rate, the way the local peasants' brains work isn't in sync with the rest of the world. Rather, they're more similar in mentality to the inhabitants of ancient Greece. In their conception, there's no heaven and hell, but rather, hell would be what Moldova is now."

"You see, there *is* hell."

"But it's not the hell of the Christian tradition. It's an ancient Greek hell, where there's no suffering, there's only nonexistence. Life being cut off—that's what terrified the ancient Greeks. Thus, they didn't have hell. And, correspondingly, no heaven either."

"Olymp—"

"A place for the gods and the elite! What's more, pious behavior in life in no way guaranteed a place in the afterlife on Olympus!"

"Interesting ..."

"In the same way, Italy is neither heaven nor hell for the local peasants. It's simply a fairytale land, where little honey islets dot the rivers, floating on waves of milk, and

Swiss cheese cliffs hang over everything. It's really cool."

"It's alright."

Octavian tossed some twigs into the fire. He turned away. "Can I ask you a very personal question?" he asked the occasional cracklings in the night.

"Go ahead," the girl answered softly. "If it's personal … "

Octavian gathered his breath and blurted out:

"Tell me, why do you torture me? I'm crazy about you, I can't live, I can't sleep. Can't breathe. I'm not asking for anything, just tell me you don't like me. I'll be happy with that. I'll live my life with that, like the Romantic hero who's satisfied with just the glove of his Beautiful Lady."

Elena was silent, and the young philologist understood that the card he'd bet everything on had turned out to be a losing one. His outburst, which had seemed to Octavian so brave and recklessly touching, had only scared the girl and turned her away. "I couldn't have waited another few years," thought the student, "so it's just as well … " He couldn't turn back in Elena's direction, otherwise he'd burn up under her mocking glance. He rubbed his hands together and, with deliberate joy, exhaled:

"Well, what do you say, time to tuck in to our tents, otherwise we'll miss out on an entire volume of fairytales tomorrow."

The girl was silent for a while. Then, "Akhrrrrr, a-khrrrr … "

Octavian couldn't believe it. He turned around. Elena was actually sleeping, snoring. The boy's fingers, shaking in humiliation, grabbed at his shirt collar and he went off to his tent. Elena lay there another twenty minutes just to be sure. The only effective way to exit a conversation, she knew, was to exit a conversation. The girl silently opened her eyes and, just in case, said one more time, "Akhrrrrrr, a-khrrrrrr."

20

"Keep in mind, sonny boy, what people say about Italy. There once was a pretty young girl who lived in these parts. She went by the name Persephona." Octavian was copying down the words of the peasant, who'd grown quite fond of the boy. Octavian was the spitting image of the old man's grandson.

"Persephone," corrected Octavian. "With an "e" at the end."

"Persephona," asserted the elder reproachfully. "It's a she, not a he. But listen. She lived without a care in the world, she didn't want for anything because her mother and father had what to live on. I mean, they were lifted up and placed on high by the communist powers. They were leaders of the collective farm and for sixteen years their daughter never lifted a finger. If she ever carried water into the house, it was the morning dew in her hair ... "

"Oh!" Octavian admired this flourish in the old man's speech. "Can you repeat that so I can copy it down accurately?"

"And if she ever carried water into the house, it was the morning dew in her hair," repeated the old man with pleasure. He'd read this turn of phrase in a literary journal once, the complete set of which was collecting dust in his basement. "Her last name was Demetrescu."

"What was that?" The student couldn't believe his own luck. "Demeter?"

"What the hell kind of Demeter?" the man said angrily. "Demetrescu was her name! Got it?"

"Yes, sir," jabbered the student. "I'm sorry, I'm writing

it down."

The peasant spun his yarn: "Well, when the Soviets left, the village began to live poorly, and Italy slowly started looking attractive to people. Nearly half the village left. And our Persephona herself was almost ready to go to Italy, but her mother, the Old Mrs. Demetrescu, wouldn't let her."

"She was afraid?"

"And how! Not a soul who'd gone to Italy had ever come back! And so Persephona Demetrescu cried for a year, then she cried for another year, because there were no suitable men left in the village. Whoever wasn't working in Italy had taken to drink, and whoever takes to drink would rather roll around with a barrel than a bride."

Breathing heavily, the old man reflected with pride on his "rather roll around with a barrel than a bride" – a phrase of his own invention. The student, holding his breath, looked at the peasant. Octavian figured he was thinking about Persephona Demetrescu.

The peasant continued: "As it happens, there arrived in these parts a representative from a tourism agency that exported our people to Italy. I reckon the company is still operating today. And the last name of that gentleman was Plutonescu."

"Pluto!" Octavian slapped his knee. "Absolutely, one hundred percent Pluto!"

"Plutonescu," the peasant corrected him angrily. "If you mean to listen, then listen! So this comrade looks at Persephona Demetrescu and loses his head over her. He starts in on offers to her parents: 'Let your daughter come with me to Italy,' he says, 'I'll set her up as a housekeeper, she'll make a thousand euros a month.' "

"Oho," said Octavian sadly. He was thinking of Elena, and of his increased scholarship of seventy-lei. That was less than five euros. "Not bad."

"And this guy, you see,"—the old man saw that the

student was transfixed by the story—"this guy spoke so slick that the girl's mother was ready to agree to the whole arrangement. But her father was against it. And they didn't let Persephona go to Italy."

"That's it?" asked Octavian. "End of story?"

"Of course not," said the old man and waved his hand. "What are you talking about? This Plutonescu character talked Persephona into running away from her father's house with him. And she, of course ... "

Octavian, who was already constructing a brilliant theory in his mind, for which fate would hand him both the Nobel Prize and the hand of Elena Syrbu, stood up and stretched. He was exultant.

"Shall I tell you what's next in this myth, grandpa?" he asked, rejoicing.

"What myth?" asked the old man. He didn't understand. "This is the pure truth, as it happened."

"Of course, of course," nodded Octavian. "Still, shall I tell you?"

"Well?" said the old man, surprised. "If you know it, why'd you write it down? If you've heard it before ... "

"I haven't heard it, but I know it," explained Octavian. This Demetrescu of yours, whom they called Persephona, she ran away from home with Plutonescu, right? They made their way to Italy slowly, slowly, and the entire time the girl's parents chased after them."

The old man opened his eyes wide and looked at the young man in disbelief. The latter, satisfied with the effect his words were having, continued.

"And so, when Persephona's parents caught sight of the runaway girl and her fugitive friend, and when they were just about to grab their daughter by the hem of her skirt, Plutonescu and Persephona traversed the symbolic boundary of hell—pardon me, I mean, the official border of Italy—and they were unreachable for the parents.

Right? The mother, seized with grief, turned to the higher gods. That is—excuse me, grandpa—to the Italian Consulate in Bucharest, demanding they return her daughter. The daughter, though – she'd gotten hitched to the old man she'd been keeping house for in Italy, and she didn't want to come back! So, the people at the consulate concocted a plan that would satisfy all parties."

"What was that?" asked the old man.

"To let Persephona leave Italy for six months, for spring and summer," said Octavian. He burst out laughing, completely happy. "But for fall and winter she'd have to return to Italy. Right?"

The old man, who'd grown completely quiet, looked at Octavian and moved farther away from the student, just in case.

"Grandsonny," he said hotly. "It wasn't like that at all. Plutonescu turned out to be a brothel keeper. And Persephona's been suffering there for some years."

Octavian, who'd been sitting still for what felt like an hour, slowly rose and went to the toilet. He threw his notebook into the cesspool. Little orange circles floated before his eyes. "This is the second blow in the last twenty-four hours. Oh, damned self-satisfaction," he thought, barely caring anymore.

"Right you are, sonny," said the old man, consoling him. "This research of yours won't do you any good. All the stories I've been telling you about, I got them from a book of mine. *Myths and Legends of Ancient Greece*. You caught on yourself. Well, I doctored the last names a little bit to fit our Moldovan ears."

"Why?" Octavian asked calmly, as he walked the dirt path back to the courtyard where the old man was. "What'd you do that for?"

The old man held up his arms. "I could tell you were looking for different stories, and lots of them. So why not help out nice folks?"

"You mean, everything's out of that book? And about Persephona?" asked Octavian with a sigh.

A gloom came over the old man's face and he poked the earth with his finger.

"About Persephona — that's the truth!" he snapped. "She's a granddaughter to me, that's how I know."

"My apologies, then. Looks like it's time for me to go." Octavian rose.

"Don't you fret," said the old man calmly, to Octavian's back. "This girlie of yours isn't meant for you, anyway. Don't you get it?"

Octavian carefully closed the gate and without paying attention to the mud, headed for the tent. He gathered his things and heated himself up some tea on the campfire. There were three hours left until the train and the young man was in no hurry.

It was evening. The dogs of Larga picked out emaciated fleas from bald spots on their coats with the occasional whimper. In the distance, a bell was ringing on a dirty sheep with a stinking wool coat. Every once in a while, the puny shepherd yelled at her. The sky was gray but transparent and from the hillock where the tents stood, it seemed a closer distance to the shepherd than to the village itself. Octavian sat with legs crossed and felt empty inside, and at the same time he felt rich. He felt all of the universe inside him, and he quietly hummed something under his breath, imagining himself to be a Medieval mullah who arrived at this place in a Turkish transport, on the way to conquering Larga. Then it seemed to him that he was an Egyptian scribe, the kind depicted on pottery displayed in the Louvre.

Suddenly the sky above Larga and the Dniester River, which snuck along somewhere nearby, became clear and rosy. It was the sun, dipping down from out of the evening clouds onto the edge of the horizon, sending the village a final salute. Octavian squinted his eyes in sweet enjoyment and caught a ray of the evening sun with his shuddering lashes. They were handsome lashes, Octavian knew. Just as he'd known since yesterday evening that Elena Syrbu meant nothing to him. And that from this day forward he'd never again study philology. What he would become in this world, Octavian didn't know. He only knew what he *wouldn't* become.

Sometime later, the distinguished member of the Russian, Moldovan, and Romanian Academies of Science, a philologist with a named professorship, Octavian Gonts, recalled that day with a thoughtful smile. He remembered it perfectly. It was the most vivid day of his life, when *something* was made clear to him. What was it? Truth? The purpose of life? Octavian was close to naming it, but he wouldn't risk giving an exact definition.

Hearing footsteps behind him, and the hard breathing of Elena, who'd climbed up onto the hill, Octavian didn't even turn around. Even though he usually ran to help her climb and lugged her heavy backpack to even ground.

"No help from you, good sir?" Elena asked him, out of breath.

Octavian's mind was still blank. With a flutter of his eyelashes he said goodbye to the sun, which had fallen off the edge of the earth, and shook his head no.

"Of course!" Elena Syrbu said mockingly. "But if I asked for a love song, it'd be a different story."

Octavian took a deep breath, glanced at his watch, stood up and started down the hill. His farewell words were: "Lug your own load, bitch!"

And when Elena, all flustered and blushing, caught up with Octavian and tried to give him a slap in the face, he grabbed hold of her by the chest and tossed her to the ground. True, he wasn't going to hit her, but he kicked her lightly with his heavy hiking boot and left for the station. The train never came, and Octavian returned to spend the night in Larga, where Elena, without answering the flurry of questions from her classmates, was lying in the tent for a sleepless night.

A year later they were married.

21

In the fall of 2003, the Moldovan priest of the village of Larga, Father Paisii, announced the First Holy Crusade of Eastern Orthodox Christians to the unclean land of Italy.

The reasons rousing the priest to this desperate act were many. But most important among them, as usual, was a lack of money. Father Paisii understood that he'd never see Italy if he had to raise the funds himself to get there. A village priest in a godforsaken parish doesn't have a shot at collecting four thousand euros. And since he couldn't pay his way to Italy, Father Paisii decided he'd have to make his way there at the head of Christ's Army. He'd read about the Crusades in seminary, where he'd been a solid C student. This decision worthy of Solomon's name came to Father Paisii not after a long discussion—he had no great love for long discussions—but in the middle of a sermon. The decision was lucid, immediate, and brief. Like a blaze, or a holy prophecy.

"My children!"

Father Paisii was delivering a sermon about Italy.

"And what is this impious country? Can it be the source of all our troubles and misfortune? There are some who will say, 'We live on the money sent to us by our loved ones from over there.' But how is this money earned? Our virtuous girls sell their bodies while our husbands, like the Israelites when they were slaves in Egypt, hang their heads and hold their tongue against their hosts, for money that means nothing to the bosses. Who gave these people the right to humiliate poor Moldovans?"

The parishioners listened to Father Paisii, who had fallen into an open-mouthed rage. The priest's sermon was becoming more and more apocalyptic.

"And does it not say in the Gospels, it is easier for a camel to pass through the eye of a needle?" asked Father Paisii, the Bible shaking in his hand. "And if it so sayeth, then why does the abominable Italy live with a full belly and contentment, while we here are impoverished, starving, and beggars all. And who, my children, who are the true Christians? The Italians, who sold themselves to that false Latin faith? No! We're the true children in Christ, and it stands to reason, everything is ours to possess. And so, let us seize everything from the impious and give it to the pious!"

The sermon was becoming more lucid and forthright. The parishioners, mouths still hanging open in amazement, began to understand what the priest was driving at. Many of them were starting to view Father Paisii with approval.

"Seize everything from the impious and give it to the pious!" The phrase rang out through the church.

Timid applause broke out from somewhere.

Father Paisii wrinkled his brow, cleared his throat and took a sip of dark wine from the gilded plastic chalice. His throat felt stuffed with cotton. The wine was dark, not because it was pressed from dark grapes. It was all because of the dust and the parishioners who couldn't pay for the services of a cleaning lady in the church. "That's why the place is a pigsty," the priest thought to himself angrily.

"We, children of God, live as in a pigsty, praying to Him just as the apostles commanded. And Italy, this Italy, which lives off the sweat of the brow of our sons and daughters—Who can say why?—this Italy grows fat and prospers. Is this fair, my children? For it says in the Bible …"

The parishioners once again grew bored. Paisii realized with relief that they didn't want him to quote more holy books, they wanted a call to action. He changed the format of his speech.

He jumped onto the ambo and in front of the holy doors. "Now hear me! Take heed, for it is not every day that the priest stands here on this holy spot. My children! We must take back that which was taken from us! Do you desire it? Answer yes, and I will lead you there, naked and proud, as Adam led Eve through the Garden of Eden until their expulsion. Do you desire it?"

"Yes!" roared the church, for who among the villagers did not want to go to Italy? And who among them had money? "We desire it!"

"I will lead you there," shouted Father Paisii and removed from beneath his cassock a sword, where he'd been keeping it for just such an occasion. He'd found the sword in an old funerary mound outside of Larga. "To slay the impure and give their wealth to the pure! Hark to my words and pass them on to your brothers and sisters, your beloved ones and your enemies. And listen, therefore ..."

White from worry, his nostrils trembling, Father Paisii waited until the ovation was finished and raised his hand again. From a corner of the church the video camera for the local television station started recording.

"This is alright," thought Paisii and waited for the red light to come on before talking.

"I am calling you to defend the true faith of God. Orthodox Christians of Moldova! The time has come for us to go to impure Italy and free our two hundred thousand countrymen, as Moses freed the Israelites from slavery in Egypt. But while Moses was unarmed, we will use force to grant our brothers freedom!"

"Hurrah!" they called out in the church. "Down with Italy!"

"I am calling for a crusade to Italy," bellowed Paisii. "Let it be so. I give you my word as a pastor, my children, that all who venture forth there, if they shall meet demise, henceforth their sins will be absolved."

"Verily!" they answered in the church, the golden flames of their candles growing fuzzy before Paisii's eyes.

"Those who would fight against their fellow believers, those who fell and those who killed their brothers in war in Transnistria—let them take up arms against the unbelievers in a battle which will bring us an abundance of spoils. We were forced to kill one another for a long time, but isn't it better to unite and attack the nonbelievers? Let the veterans take up arms."

"I-ta-ly, I-ta-ly!!!!

"That land flows with milk and honey," said Paisii, brandishing his sword. "He who once was a thief, shall be a warrior today. Whoever has done battle with his fellow believer: Come with me!"

"Yes!!!"

"Whoever here is wretched, shall be wealthy there! And so, my children, tomorrow we take up arms."

"As God desires!"

The far-off shouts of the crowd mixed into one regular rumble. Later, Father Paisii fearfully admitted in his heart that amongst the howls and the noise he clearly heard somebody's subdued shout, "Goal!" He even heard somebody emit a cheer for the Chisinau soccer team. The one thing Paisii, grandson of a Jew, did not hear was a cry of "Kill the Jews!" He let out a sigh of relief.

That evening they carried the priest home on their shoulders. It was a true triumph for Paisii. His terrified kiddies watched as their father was carried into the courtyard. Afterwards, the people dispersed to prepare for the crusade, while the priest barely made it to the front door on his wobbly legs. After he had calmed down, Paisii sharpened his already-sharp knife—"Too bad the blade's a bit short," he thought—and grabbed a massive cross. He threw together a bag of provisions. He gave a slap on

the withers to the young mare he was planning on traveling with and caught a few winks. In his dreams he saw
miraculous vineyards in Italy which he, Paisii, would pass
on to his children in a chain of eternal possession, after
the crusade had ended in complete and definitive victory
for the holy warriors of Moldova. In his dreams he saw
the full, milky white arms of his runaway wife, like those
shameless Madonnas in the Italian frescoes …

At six in the morning, Paisii had somewhat recovered from
the dark wine in the plastic chalice and was tormented by
thoughts of the future shame this day would bring him.
At seven, waking up for good, Paisii rubbed his eyes a
minute, went out into the yard and smiled awkwardly and
confusedly. The priest was in shock.

Surrounding his house was a well-armed crowd, heav-
ing, holding their religious banners. There were seventy-
five thousand people from across Moldova. Upon catching sight of Father Paisii, the crowd applauded. Old Man
Tudor brought Paisii his little horsie and hefted him
up onto the saddle. As if watching a sporting event at
a stadium, the crowd gave him a real welcome: they did
the wave. The priest sensed another, warm type of wave,
one which swelled up through his breast to his heart and
which he couldn't hold back. His tears were warm as a
mother's hands.

Tudor put on a Romanian infantry helmet from World
War Two. "Verily, it's unbecoming for us, old men-at-
arms, to cry. Wipe away the tears and lead us to Italy,
Lord!"

22

Of the origins of the First Moldovan Crusade, it is possible to note several interesting moments of extreme import. First among them is the disarray of the crusading army. Amidst an atmosphere of general confusion, the great leader, Father Paisii, commanded the soldiers to traverse the cities and towns of Moldova in a peaceful march until Chisinau, the leader of the crusade intending to take the Icon of the Mother of God of Three Hands, and advance with the object to Italy. Paisii said, without the icon our undertaking was doomed to failure. (It was doomed to fail anyway, but then I am getting ahead of the story.) Such was the official explanation.

I, a Chronicler following his army, had been in the secular world a teacher in the village of Larga who left his position for lack of demand, as the school was closed. I suggest different motives. It seems to me that Paisii, the leader of our ill-fated exploits, simply did not expect such a number of people as thronged together under his banner. In the Balti region alone, whither the Army of Christ arrived, there joined with us fifteen thousand local residents. All of whom accepted our apothem with enthusiasm: "To Italy! Such is God's will!"

I will cite dry numbers. In the Orhei region, from the village of Grozdeshti, where the population is 345, the number of residents who joined us was 345. All of Grozdeshti, from young to old, came with us. In total, the Orhei region gave us 21,000 warriors, men and women. In the Soroki region, 10,000 local gypsies bonded with us saying, "We are tired of a life of alms collecting in trains and want a different, better life ..."

We accepted all, and perhaps we acted mistakenly, for in the third month of our crusade there began thievery and violence. To our misfortune, the troops of Saint Paisii our Father advanced very slowly. Toward the third month we were but twenty-five miles away from Chisinau, having advanced in that time only ten miles. The movement of the crusaders was much delayed for many of our number were on foot, and we waited for them. Likewise we waited for the infants, accompanied by their mothers in the caravans, happy maidens following after the caravans, and the constant trials with the local population were also a nuisance.

But the army and the police dared not touch us, since in Moldova there are 9,000 soldiers, officers and generals, and 20,000 policemen. And at the time in question, during the First Moldovan Crusade, we were already 126,000 souls. A third of us were infirm, women with children, or old men, nonetheless we were a body and they were afraid of us and did not lay their hands upon us. And many policemen even joined with us, saying, "What use is it to stay at home and risk my life, only to receive a hundred dollars a month, if in Italy I can make a thousand euros just for washing dishes?" And so we grew exceedingly in number, to the delight of the army, praise be to God, Amen.

Having taken upon myself the responsibility of attesting to what befell us, I say, as the Chronicler of the Crusade, that at the end of the third month the local residents were more poorly disposed to us, and looked upon us with increasing displeasure.

In the beginning the residents of Moldova joined the ranks of our army with fervor, but at the end of the third month they began to place obstacles in our way and even tried to halt our procession. They called us marauders, robbers and swindlers. And faithful were their words, for too numerous were the dishonest folk who joined our Holy Crusade to godless Italy. Father Paisii himself, intending to pass the winter

The Good Life Elsewhere

in Moldova as the army was not ready to overtake Europe, understood however that if we did not venture beyond the borders of our country, the crusade would end in a disaster, all at once ... And Father Paisii, having taken counsel with the Lord, went out to the people and told them we were retreating from Chisinau and making our way to the smaller western city of Ungheni. From there, we would sail to Romania. And he lifted his sharpened sword, which had once belonged to the Emperor Trajan, saying:

"Follow me, my children!"

And a flame of ecstasy blazed up again in our hearts, which had gone cold from delays and procrastination. Even the bandits became holy, the prostitutes were cured of their lust and the swindlers returned the stolen goods. The muggers and violent offenders singed their own hands that had committed evil. And so we moved forward, and in Ungheni there poured into our army another 10,000 souls, and they all desired, like us, from the first to the last, only one thing.

To go to Italy. To God.

23

Father Paisii's sword, recorded in Moldovan history as the "Sword of Father Paisii" and the "Sword of Emperor Trajan of Rome," was forged from the steel shocks of a truck. Thus, the "Sword of Emperor Trajan" had never really belonged to the Emperor, at all.

"It's a forgery," said the best goldsmith in Ungheni, who also happened to be an antique lover. Luckily, unlike many other residents, he hadn't abandoned the city with the approach of the crusaders.

"A clever forgery, but pretty unsophisticated. As you can see, the sword maker didn't even erase the inscription that says, 'Engineering Works.' "

"Is that so?" Paisii was absentmindedly biting his lip. He'd really come into his own during the course of the crusade. "I wasn't expecting that …"

The goldsmith looked at Paisii with a grin, giving the sword a toss in his hand. It was shaped liked the Scythian *acinaces*, but was there anybody else there who knew a thing about history? The goldsmith sighed. Shouts were coming from the street. It was the crusading army, pillaging the city. Downtown Ungheni was in flames. With shouts of "Italy, Europe, Heaven!" the pilgrims were dragging couches and television sets out of abandoned houses. Paisii wiped his pale temples. He knew that the couches were being adapted into carriages, and he wasn't surprised.

"Just think," said the goldsmith, shrugging his shoulders. "The twenty-first century, and look what's happening. I can't believe it."

"Believe it," answered Paisii coldly. "You're a man of a meticulous craft. These are the facts. You better come to grips with them."

The goldsmith winked. "Any nominally trained army, even from a backwards country like Romania, or even Slovenia, will wipe you out."

And the seasoned Paisii, who had indeed "grown exceedingly wise" as a result of leading the vast army of pilgrims, as the chronicler noted, smiled.

"I'm counting on them letting us be. For the same reason they let the Albanians alone." The priest gave a cunning wink, like a mischievous boy.

"Which is?" asked the goldsmith, confused.

The priest smiled even wider.

"Do whatever you want, as long as you say you want to be a part of Europe. And then you'll get away with anything. Look, the Albanians do God knows what. They sell weapons and women, they take hostages. And the world forgives them, as long as they're pro-Europe and pro-NATO. They'll forgive us, too. That's the trend in today's world."

"The exception being this." The goldsmith shook his head. "Barbarians like you and the Albanians – Europe lets them do whatever they want, but only in certain, specific places. Italy, alas, isn't one of them."

"Well, they've already shot three stories about us for *EuroNews* and written dozens of articles in the European papers," said the priest, now unsure of himself. "They all praise us for striving toward the democratic world and shaking off the dust of our communist past."

"Which is what they'll do until the exact hour when your army of—excuse me—ragamuffins shows up at the border of the European Union. Then they'll stop being so welcoming," explained the goldsmith.

"You don't mean they won't take us?" said Paisii, now thrown into doubt. "No, impossible … "

"They won't take you," the goldsmith cautiously warned. "Now, if you were to lead a crusade to Russia, they'd support you to the end. But when you're talking about Europe itself, they don't need riffraff like you."

"What do you know about it?" said Paisii, putting the brakes on the argument. "Better, let's take care of the sword. I would like for it to be the sword of Emperor Trajan."

"Uh, if you'll allow me," said the goldsmith, very delicately. "How's that? Erase the inscription?"

Paisii looked at the inscription pensively—truly, it'd be a sin to just ignore it—and he patted the goldsmith on the cheek. With his sword.

"No. Leave it. Just engrave two more words above the inscription," he said, after a long pause. "The Emperor's title and his name. Then, the sword will no longer be a forgery."

The goldsmith swallowed his soupy saliva. "And then what'll we be left with?" he whispered.

"Emperor Trajan's Engineering Works!"

24

**MOLDOVAN CITIZEN DETAINED BY PO-
LICE ON CHARGES OF HUMAN TRAFFICK-
ING.** A Moldovan citizen was detained by the police
on charges of organizing passage for hopeful émigrés.
Sources inside the Ministry of Interior have informed
Moldova Independent Press of these goings on.

32-year-old Chisinau native Valeriu Albu, together
with accomplices from Romania, Serbia, Croatia,
and Slovenia, organized a route of transport for
Moldovan citizens seeking to work illegally in Italy.

Under questioning, Albu confessed to enlisting
around 100 Moldovan citizens, receiving from
them a total of 90,600 Euros. Upon arrival, the unsuspecting people were not given employment, as
they had been promised by the enterprising swindlers. Instead, they were detained and held in captivity. Realizing they had been duped, the people
surrendered themselves to the Croatian police and
were deported back to Moldova.

REMAINS OF ROMAN EMPORER TRAJAN'S ENGINEERING WORKS UNCOVERED IN MOLDOVA. The surprising discovery was made by researcher Jan Byzgu, who studies the peaceful coexistence of the cultures of the Roman Empire and Dacia. Soviet historians mistakenly referred to the period as the "Roman occupation of Dacia." According the researcher, it was not an occupation, but rather a fruitful collaboration between two cultures.

Attesting to this are the unique discoveries made by Byzgu at the end of last month outside of Ungheni. In a nearby town, thanks to the prompting of local residents, the location of what seems to be the first Daco-Roman engineering works was uncovered.

"Of course," said the researcher, the excitement audible in his voice, "they weren't producing submarines. But we are aware of the existence of one surviving artifact from this factory, a Roman sword, with an engraving: "Engineering Works of Emperor Trajan.""

As the researcher told this agency, the sword belonged to the leader of the World March for European Integration, mistaken by Romanian border troops as Father Paisii's Holy Crusade (see article under headline 40,000 MOLDOVAN CITIZENS DROWN IN PRUT RIVER UPON ILLEGAL CROSSSING INTO ROMANIA, 02.12.2004 / 08:33). Father Paisii spoke with a correspondent from our agency:

"Unfortunately, the sword drowned in the Prut River. Thank God, I didn't drown, too. Now this

The Good Life Elsewhere

sword is lying on the riverbed, uniting us with Mother Romania, as an eternal reproach to our neighbors."

It is noteworthy, the researcher further argued, that the inscription on the sword was engraved in the Romanian language, and, consequently, we see that Latin was actually Romanian, and not the invented language that for many centuries has passed for ancient Latin.

Today, what's left of Emperor Trajan's engineering works in present-day Moldova are a pit, several structures in half-ruin which the local population mistakenly took for neglected pigpens from the former collective farm on the same spot, and stone structures which appear to be walls of some sort. In the near future the site will be visited by President Voronin for the opening of a Historical Heritage Site.

We also relate that at the time of the discovery, the researcher himself, Jan Byzgu, was participating in the March for Europe & the World, also known as the first Moldovan Holy Crusade (see article from Moldova Independent Press Agency on 01.12.2004 / 05:38 and 10.17.2003 / 07:38). The march is being led by Moldovan enthusiasts, supporters of the European path for Moldovan integration into the EU and the repudiation of cooperation with Russia and the Commonwealth of Independent States.

25

AFTER GIVING THE CITY OVER TO FIRE AND SWORD, OUR VALIANT pilgrims sat down to rest in Ungheni Park, which extends to the border, that is, to the Prut River. And the whole night we were able to observe the fires burning on the other bank, and even in the Romanian city of Iasi, which did not slumber. At midnight there arrived at our camp a delegation from the Romanian parliament, who told us they would not let our army pass. Although Father Paisii promised peace and security, saying, "Our mission is only to reach the impious Italy, you shall render us assistance and let us pass in peace."

But the cunning Romanian envoys refused our demand, saying Romania is already a member of the European Union and thus obliged to protect its borders. And notwithstanding their impudent speech, they were peacefully released by us and by our leader, Father Paisii. And he delivered a speech before us, and I, the Chronicler of this, the first Holy Moldovan Crusade, transmit it here with some abridgment, for Father Paisii said much that was incoherent. For he, like the entire army, had drunk adequately. During the pillaging of Ungheni the devil brought under our control an entire wine and vodka works.

"Brothers, hear my speech," Paisii spoke. "Romania does not desire Moldovan pilgrims upon its borders. But they will be helpless before us if we are in Romania, having passed through their country peaceably. They will not smite us, for we will be carrying high the banner of our yearning for European integration. Thus, most important is to cross the river and, gathering together in one column, to walk straight and strong, with God in our hearts!"

And our ears rejoiced and many did not close their eyes until morning, for they were drunk and excited. And toward morning many fell silent, for they were on the cusp of their dreams, and all that remained to do was take a step and soar, as fledglings. And on the opposite bank of the river they had put out their fires, for the Romanians decided we would delay our crossing. And our leader Father Paisii struck his sword at the fourth hour of the morning, when the slumber of the border guards was heavy, and thus gave a sign for the crossing.

Alas and alack, to our misfortune. Our army was not well intentioned in their hearts and God destroyed our plans, effortlessly and easily, though not as a young boy destroys a fortress built of toy blocks, but as a stern father destroys the impious Tower of Babylon. And the entire river was overfilled with vessels large and small, though the width of the crossing in that place did not attain even fifty meters. Because of the clustering of people, a crush began, and many descended to the riverbed. Their steel armor sank, to multiply our misfortune. And verily, many drowned because they did not want to part with the loot they had stolen in Ungheni, and even earlier in Calarasi.

And mothers wailed, their eyes following their drowning young children, and the men swam, trying to save themselves, but mercy was not theirs to own. The current of the Prut in that place exactly is very quick and it drags a swimmer down to the bottom with more strength than God dragged Jonah to the fulfillment of his destiny.

And one soul in four had drowned, for the wind was increasing and many sloops were overturned, and a battalion of Romanian border guards tore asunder with a barrage of accurate bullets those who were not fated to drown. And so yet again one in four souls of our pilgrims were shot. Or, being wounded and without strength, they drowned. And Father Paisii was wounded, and he let fall the sword of Em-

peror Trajan into the river, and this holy weapon drowned. And of those ten thousand that ascended to the Romanian side, afterwards it was heard that they were sold to the Albanians. The Albanians separated the people and sold them once again. The men were sent to the snake-infested orange groves of Greece where, if they were not felled by poisonous bites, the sun would surely strike them. And the women were sold to Kosovo, where they were used by peacekeeping troops. And we, the survivors, cried to see how they were led away on the opposite bank. And the twenty thousand who remained from the entire crusading army were scattered by cold and hunger. And we returned to our villages across Moldova, to eke out a miserable existence and save money.

For every one among us still dreamed of leaving to go work in Italy.

26

It took Vasily Lungu and Serafim Botezatu nearly a month to reach home. Because of the tractor, they couldn't make it any faster: for an entire one hundred and twenty miles they lugged its remains. The men walked along the railroad tracks; the trains were forced to wait patiently while they dragged themselves from one station to another. When passengers realized that right before there eyes passed not just two random men, but Vasily and Serafim in the flesh, those two men who'd tried to fly a tractor to Italy—they'd been written up in the all the newspapers—they gave the travelers a standing ovation. The only ones who didn't share the people's joy were the conductors, the train and tram drivers, and the stationmasters.

"Come on, can't you drag yourselves any faster?" the railroad men shouted nervously, letting off steam from their engines and getting hot between the ears themselves. "Get off the tracks, you pests."

"Let them alone," the passengers interceded on behalf of the men. "They're chasing after their dreams. If their dreams are slow as molasses, so be it."

The railroad men resigned themselves and hit the breaks. They ran the trains at the lowest speed and plodded along dejectedly behind Vasily and Serafim, every now and then nipping at their tails. The passengers would exit the wagons to stretch their legs and breathe in the fresh air. They held picnics and weren't afraid of being left behind, for in an entire hour the train would only cover a mile or two, no more. Many people sunbathed on the roof, and the especially impatient women manipulated sunbeams that bounced off their makeup mirrors. They'd stop only for a passionate kiss.

"It's so nice that there are men like Serafim Botezatu and Vasily Lungu in this world," the ladies said exultantly. "Thanks to them, we remember that we needn't always hurry. And thanks to them, time comes to a standstill, like when a dog is chasing after a bird and suddenly he gets a whiff of a bone buried in the ground ... "

And Vasily and Serafim walked on, straining their backs, dripping the sweat of their exhaustion onto the scorching rails, and smiling unhappily to each other. Both mulled over the fact that had they not fallen asleep, they might have evaded the Grad missile that blasted through the clouds where their flying tractor was hiding. But such was their fate. They both understood, and Vasily no longer held out hope for anything, since his entire life had been wrecked along with the tractor.

"And the reason we're carrying the remains of this machine back to Larga," he'd explain, huffing and puffing, to Serafim—who hadn't asked why they were carrying the remains of the machine back to Larga, but was simply doing so out of obedience—"is to return the remains to the earth, like the body of the finest of men."

Vasily firmly resolved to bury his flying tractor close to his father, a good man, hallowed be his name, whose heart had been softer than a melting ice rose. Remembering this, he perked up his step and encouraged his fellow traveler.

"Ekh, Serafim," he would smile, crying. "We wouldn't have been able to face ourselves if we hadn't tried to make it to Italy. But obviously, it wasn't meant to be. And if that's the case, why battle fate?"

"Let's talk about it later, after we get to Larga and have some rest," Serafim said sharply. He was hatching new plans.

The steam engine behind them gave out a mighty whistle and the friends, lifting their heads, saw another train coming toward them. The two engineers shook their fists and shouted at each other, while the friends dragged themselves along the line and exchanged bows to the passengers' applause.

They wrote about Vasily and Serafim in the newspapers – initially in the railway papers and then in the national news. They called them "pilgrims of the rails." At first, the Moldova Railroad administration wanted to clear them off the lines, since they'd caused a four-day delay in the train schedule. But when they saw the popularity the friends enjoyed, the administration decided they could use the situation to their advantage. They offered Vasily and Serafim steady work: to ride the line back and forth from Chisinau to Ungheni. The bureaucrats were planning on launching five luxury trains along the route, complete with saunas, movie cars, dance cars, restaurants, swimming pools, libraries, and deluxe berths. They were going to charge three hundred dollars a ticket for a ride on the proposed route, and attract foreign passengers. They planned on calling the tour "Charm of the Railroad, or Philosopher of the Rails."

But while they were searching for start-up capital, Vasily and Serafim had taken the branch line to Ungheni and then climbed north, making their way back to Larga. During the course of their journey, they'd become the darlings of all the train passengers of Moldova. But never once did they step inside a wagon.

They couldn't afford a ticket.

27

After a week of catching up on sleep, Serafim awoke at dawn. His eyes followed the fading Morning Star in the shimmering blue of the new day and he thought about how to get to Italy. He washed up and hurried to Vasily's house.

"Vasily, wake up!" He shook his friend awake. "I've figured out how to get to Italy!"

Vasily, who'd been sleeping on a wooden bench underneath the walnut tree, blinked long and tried to understand what was going on. And when he figured out what Serafim wanted, Lungu fell into deep thought and climbed out from under the blanket.

"Some things you can't talk about with a dry mouth," he said grandly. "Got to give the brain a boost!"

And slipping his bare feet into his old galoshes, he went into the basement for some wine from the best harvest – made from the grapes he'd gathered with his now-deceased wife. They had lived together peacefully that fall, and for that reason the wine always bore a hint of the unbearable bitterness of Maria's later tears. Which is why Vasily liked it so much.

"You understand, we're going to need materials for this," he said to Serafim before drinking the first round.

"I realize," Serafim answered with restraint. "Drink."

"And now you," said Vasily, handing his friend the glass and taking a whiff of the crumbled walnut leaf he had in his hand. "Where are we gonna get the materials without any money? Are we gonna *steal* the money?"

"No point in that," answered Serafim logically. "If we stole the money, why waste it on materials? We could just spend it on a trip to Italy."

"Well put," Vasily agreed. "So?"

"You know, to implement this grand plan we'll need a submarine," began Serafim, pensively. "Not too large, something we can swim out of the Dniester in and cross over to the Black Sea, go around the coast of Romania and Bulgaria, and set our course straight for Italy."

"Right." Vasily shook his head. "But you can't make a submarine out of thin air."

"We'll make it out of materials." Serafim gave the walnut tree a once-over and poured wine reflexively. "Out of materials, my friend."

"What do you mean?" Vasily couldn't contain himself any longer. "We haven't got a pot to piss in!"

Serafim paused for dramatic effect, drank his wine down, looked at Vasily from over his glass, passed it to his friend, and said, positively:

"We'll dig up the remains of the tractor!"

28

OF COURSE, AT FIRST THE FRIENDS FOUGHT. VASILY, AL-most immediately upon hearing Serafim's blasphemous suggestion, drove his leg into his friend's chest, and when Serafim fell, he went running for his pitchfork. Coming back from the barn fully armed, Vasily shook his head, be-cause the offender had simply disappeared. True, he wasn't lost for long, and jumped straight onto Vasily's head from a branch of the walnut tree. Serafim beat Vasily's head off the bench until his friend saw red stars. Then, without crawling out from under Serafim, Vasily punched him in the side.

"Ekh," Serafim said, doubled over from the blow. "Ekh, ekh."

Meanwhile, Vasily hit him in the back with the blunt end of the pitchfork, and the only reason he used the blunt end was that he was holding the pitchfork in an un-comfortable position, and by the time he spun it around to use as a skewer, Serafim had hurled a pitcher of wine at his face and pulled a terribly effective move. The move was one the friends had seen back when they were still kids in the dawn of the nineties, and the collective farm had screened the movies of Bruce Lee. Those were the days when you'd have to pay three rubles for entrance into a room that had a VCR. Jumping up high and grabbing onto the branch of the walnut tree, Serafim thrust both legs into Vasily's chest.

"Hi-ya!" he yelled.

After which, he prudently grabbed the pitchfork and took shelter in the house. Serafim was saved from arson only because it was Vasily's house, and Vasily couldn't bring himself to burn down his own place of residence, even to smoke out a newly acquired enemy.

29

TOWARD MIDNIGHT THE WINE RAN OUT IN THE HOUSE AND Serafim began to cry and ask to be let out. Vasily lightened up after five jugs of wine and the friends reconciled, sealing their friendship with a sturdy kiss and a manly embrace.

"And now," said Serafim, wiping away a tear, "let's go see the priest. If he sang the requiem service and returned the remains of the tractor to the earth in a Christian way, then surely he'll agree to carry out this *waddayacallit*, this exhumation."

The month before, Father Paisii, finding himself in very difficult financial straits, had indeed agreed to carry out the requiem rites over the scraps of steel Vasily and Serafim had brought to the village. The priest had even read out, "Then shall the dust of the servant of God, the tractor, return to the earth." But would Paisii, who'd already once committed a perversion of the Christian doctrine, agree to repeat his sacrilege? Serafim had no doubts he would. Vasily wasn't quite as sure, but he didn't care to chance another all-day bloodbath with his pal, since his head still ached from the wine and his ribs from the punches.

"What?" cried the shocked Paisii, leaning out the window. "Dig up the deceased?"

"Father," said Serafim, trying to assuage the situation, "it's just a machine, after all. A tractor."

"What difference does it make?" hissed Paisii. After we gave it a Christian burial, that tractor of yours became like any other normal dead person. Unbury the deceased?

Have you lost your mind?"

"Please, kind Father, we really need this. It's for a righteous cause," Vasily entreated.

"No," answered Father Paisii, definitely. "If you even try, I'll excommunicate you. You've lost all your marbles. At first you force the priest to sing the requiem over your tractor, then you ask the priest for permission to dig up this dead – I mean, to dig up this tractor! Tfu!"

"Father!"

"Heretics!"

"Father Paisii!"

"I'll excommunicate you. Don't even ask. Got it? Do you know what the crux of our religion is?

"What?" asked Vasily, utterly baffled.

"Our religion is the sword," uttered Paisii, "for it is said, 'I did not come to bring peace, but a sword.'"

And it was here that Vasily interrupted.

"And what if we send you a visa invitation from Italy?" he asked quietly. "An invitation and a job. We'll give it to you in writing."

The priest exhaled loudly through his nose and sat down on the windowsill.

"Our religion," said Paisii, stretching out an arm holding pen and paper to his friends, "is peace and mercy. Start writing."

30

In the presence of a handful of villagers and the priest, who'd given his blessing to the procedure, the friends dug up the tractor's grave and took down the marker from the cross. On the marker was inscribed:

KOLKHOZ COMMUNAL TRACTOR
IN REMEMBRANCE AND LOVE
1980-2004

The grave marker also contained a drawing of a tractor. The tractor had a human hand. The human hand had a glass of wine. Now the need for such a memorial had passed.

"I bless you," Paisii pronounced quickly, crossing the friends, "and remember, good Christians keep their word."

And he left, his dirty cassock sweeping up the cemetery dust in his haste. Vasily, watching him leave, thought the priest was clearly up to something.

Serafim huffed and puffed as he dismantled the coffin where, a month ago, Vasily had wanted to bury the tractor remains. "The motor can't be repaired, but it doesn't matter. We'll need it for ballast. And we can use the metal for the body."

In the end, the priest ducked behind the churchyard fence and Vasily lent Serafim a hand. Within an hour they'd managed pretty well. They placed the empty coffin in the shed in the corner of the cemetery, and they carried the

The Good Life Elsewhere

tractor remains by wheelbarrow back to Vasily's house. Along the way the friends began to argue about how the submarine would look, what color they'd paint it and what they were going to call it. But they kept themselves in check, limiting their argument to verbal jousting.

"In any case," sighed Vasily, "we've got to do something about a motor. If we try to sail to Italy using only the underwater current pattern, it'll take us over a year to reach our goal."

"There won't be any problems with the motor," said Serafim, calming his friend. "Just take a look over there."

Vasily raised his eyes and saw before his eyes the bicycle of Old Man Tudor; specifically, the pedals. He understood everything.

31

Vasily, in a splendid black uniform, with golden threading on his peaked cap and bright red stripes down the sides of his trousers, was standing at attention. Next to him, stooping slightly—which only proved he'd never served in the army—was Serafim, looking askance and slightly craning his neck. Both of them were giving the once-over to the Romanian border guard, who'd nearly lost the gift of speech upon seeing these two strange Moldovans. Usually, it was people in their cars who passed through this checkpoint. But these two had arrived on foot, and not empty-handed, either. Not that they had cigarettes, instant coffee, or pork, which Moldovans usually transported to Iasi to peddle. These two were hauling a strange sort of creation in their arms, something that looked an awful lot like a cheap cigar, or ...

"A submarine!" whispered the border guard, barely able to believe his eyes. "A small, but damned if-it-ain't submarine! Jesus Christ. What will these Moldovans do next, huh? Are they planning on hawking that small thing in Iassi?"

Shaking his head in disbelief, the Romanian watched as the two strange birds approached the checkpoint. And if their lugging a submarine weren't enough, they also happened to be decked out like jesters. One was an admiral without a fleet, the other, in his striped sailor's vest and pirate's bandana on his good-for-nothing noggin ...

"Oh boy, again with the nutcases?" he thought.

"Here you are," said Serafim, practically luminous, handing his accompanying documents to the border guard. "Kindly have a look."

He stood straight at attention next to Vasily. Tongues sticking out of their mouths from the heat, both of them yearned to have a seat in the shadow of the customs booth and let the breeze blow through their beards. Alas, that space was occupied by several stray dogs, whom the agents fed and whom they allowed to crisscross over the government border whenever the animals felt like it. The guard tsk-tsked, scratched his sun-frazzled hair, and began to read:

"An unusual competition is under way in the American state of Maryland, where engineering students are demonstrating their pedal-operated homemade submarines. The winning team will sail a distance of a hundred meters in their vessel in the shortest time. The tournament is taking place in special US Navy training waters," stammered the agent, reading the piece of paper. "According to participants, the requirements for victory include innovative submarine construction – and strong legs."

Vasily and Serafim smiled and nodded.

"What in God's name is this?" asked the Romanian in surprise.

"This," said Serafim, pointing to the piece of paper he'd ripped out of the newspaper, "is a document confirming our participation in an international competition that's going to take place in the United States. We'll be there as honorary guests."

"And how are you going to get to the States? On foot?" The agent, so flabbergasted by the insolence of the Moldovans, couldn't even muster anger.

"By sea," Vasily said, looking pityingly at the Romanian. "Isn't that obvious?"

Taking a deep breath, the agent stood his ground for a minute, fastened up his guard jacket with the high collar, adjusted his cap and saluted the two crazy Moldovans. He spun around precisely, as if on a parade ground, and marched straight to the booth, where, choking with laughter, he told his colleagues everything. They'd been following the scene out of boredom. The men picked themselves up, stretched themselves out, and went to meet Vasily and Serafim, as if attending a grand ceremony.

The commanding officer bit his lip.

"We're happy to welcome such valiant representatives of what, without a doubt, is the embryo of the great nascent naval fleet of Moldova."

32

"Do you think Old Man Tudor will forgive us for stealing his bicycle?" Vasily asked as he lazily pedaled their contraption.

"Not his *bicycle*," Serafim corrected him. "Just the *pedals*." He was charting their course through the small Plexiglass window he'd filched from the office of the regional land surveyor's office.

"We stole the entire *bicycle*!" Vasily said testily.

"But we only *took* the pedals," objected Serafim. "There's a difference."

"No, there isn't," Vasily decided, thinking on it for a while. "If a fox strangles a goose just to eat the brains, you wouldn't say the fox killed the brains. You'd say the fox offed the goose."

"If your conscience is bothering you because of Old Man Tudor's bicycle, it shouldn't." There was a note of understanding in Serafim's voice and he clapped his friend on the shoulder. "When we get to Italy and make heaps of money, we'll buy him the best racing bike there is, you can be sure of that. And we'll send him the bicycle along with a heap of money."

"And the old one?" Vasily asked nervously, anxiously. "What'll happen with the old one? It's not completely ready for the scrap heap. You can't waste all that good hardware!"

"We'll put the bicycle without pedals into the Larga Village Museum, when we get as rich as Croesus," Serafim promised grandly. We'll put our submarine there, too. Schoolchildren will feast their eyes on our submarine and our bicycle!"

"It's not *our* bicycle, but Old Man Tudor's, to be exact," said Vasily.

"What's the difference, anyway?"

"And, by the way, as soon as our sudmarine ..."

"A sudmarine is what you get when you drop your soap in the sea," said Serafim. He made a sour face. "What we've got is a *sub*marine. Got it? Remember. *SUB*marine."

"I got it. So, when our submarine floats to ... "

Serafim interrupted viciously: "Floating is for feces that get taken by the waves. A submarine cruises. Got it? Remember. A submarine cruises. Remember that. Submarine. Cruises."

"You're a real sea dog," said Vasily with respect. "Where'd you manage to pick it all up?"

"From books," Serafim admitted, "like just about everything else I know in life. I learned the Italian language and the country from books, I fell in love with Michelangelo's sculptures thanks to books. You can tell, I haven't actually seen or heard anything firsthand in this life."

"Your love for Italy is worthy of the greatest respect," said Vasily approvingly. "But where did you find a book to teach yourself Italian?"

Serafim took a deep breath and his head sagged. Grey hairs shone atop his head, just like the occasional ray of sunshine that bounced off the dark waters of the river. And for a brief moment Vasily admired the profile of his friend, now pensive and gloomy.

"We're leaving the estuary," said Serafim quietly. "In a minute we'll be on the open sea. Don't push the pedals too hard. We don't want to stray too far from shore."

Vasily nodded and let up on the pedals. As he glanced at his surroundings, he was surprised at his own engineering genius. A small submarine, encased in metal panels taken from a long-suffering tractor, with an interior like a comfortable little closet. The two men were quartered quite freely inside. Besides the two seats—for the captain and his oarsman—there were deck chairs set up for relaxation. A retractable pipe had also been put in, which, in case of an accident, would let in air. Vasily smiled. Everything was going according to plan.

"Don't get too comfy," Serafim warned him. "We've got lots of work to do. It was the current that carried us to the estuary, but we won't have such luck in the sea."

Toward midnight the friends brought the vessel to the surface and heaved to. Vasily stared at the warm stars of the estuary, still native and Moldovan, but already nearly Ukrainian and thus, almost foreign. He daydreamed, letting his hand down into the warm water.

And Serafim was watching the path the moon's reflection made in the water. It reminded him of Stella's hair.

33

FLYING PAST THE ALPS, THE AIRPLANE TOOK A STEEP TURN and the president heard a whistling in his ears. After waiting for the aircraft to straighten out, he got up from his seat, ignoring the stewardesses' request, and walked into the cockpit.

"Can't you take it easy? You've flipped your lids, dog-fighters," he shouted.

"Sorry, Mister President, but in order to disappear from the radar, that was an absolutely necessary trick," the pilots explained.

President Voronin grumbled a minute longer, then took a seat directly on the floor and sipped tea from a thermos. "Some cognac in here would be nice," the president thought. But that would come later, he decided. At his age, risky procedures like this one ought to be carried out stone-cold sober.

"Some cognac," thought the pilot, licking his lips. He'd read his boss's mind. "I'll get drunk later."

The president surveyed his surroundings. In the cabin, twenty members of his retinue crowded in the aisle. Five advisers, six people from the Office of Protocol, one Minister of Reintegration and eight complete strangers. These had joined the presidential delegation simply because they'd come up with four thousand euros for the trip to Italy. Also on board were two men whose fate was unclear: an economic advisor and a political advisor on domestic affairs; Voronin was not overly fond of the latter.

"Fellows, everything will go off without a hitch?" Voronin asked. "You'll smash the plane to bits, right?"

The young pilots with their toothy grins smiled. "To smash a plane just a little bit, Mister President, isn't really possible. So we'll smash it to bits. Don't worry. Have you got your parachute?"

"Yes, Sir!" answered Voronin, suddenly in military mode, and again he felt a yen for cognac. "Have you got what to drink? For later, I mean. On the ground."

"It stands to reason!"

The flyers chuckled and Voronin felt relieved. Only ten minutes until the realization of his dreams. Two minutes ago his plane had dropped off earth's radar. Now they were already flying above Italian territory. In five minutes he and his retinue—everybody who'd contributed four thousand euros—would jump with their parachutes. Some Moldovans who were in the business of setting up work for their countrymen in Italy would be waiting for them at an agreed-upon point.

"Finally," Voronin said to himself, "I'm going to a normal country. Where the streets are clean. Where people are polite. Where everybody lives like they're in paradise. Maybe," he thought, feeling inside his jacket lining for the ten thousand euros sewn in there, "I'll open a pizzeria someday.

"Meanwhile, let Speaker Lupu sort things out back home. He's young, he'll figure things out. And anyway," Voronin reasoned, "no matter who comes to power in that country, nobody can improve things. Moldova is doomed. So to hell with it!

"In ten minutes," his thoughts went, "I'll jump with this parachute, they'll be waiting for me, they'll bring me to a village in the north of Italy, give me documents and a job. And my whole retinue will get the same treatment. After the pilots jump, the airplane will crash into the summit of the mountains. And in the weeks before anybody finds it, it'll be covered with snow and ice, and it's doubtful they'll even search for the bodies." The president saw the plan come together as a whole and again marveled at the minds of those who map out these little crossings of Moldovans into Italy. If more of them went into government, maybe Moldova would see its way out!

"So, you're the president?"

The man in the Chisinau office had pensively spun Voronin's business card in his hands.

"And you want to hightail it to Italy, but you've only got four thousand euros? Well, what's the problem? That happens to be our normal fee. You don't want to go by bus? Then how? Let's think, how can we ship you? There's just one condition."

"Sure, sure," the president had eagerly replied.

He arrived to the office in the evening. He'd found the firm by an announcement pasted onto a telephone pole. The announcement read: "We'll send you to Italy. Legitimate, fully-clothed activity." And two telephone numbers.

"The condition is simple," said the businessman. "Gas is on you."

Voronin laughed when he thought about the mug of mourning Berlusconi would slap onto his face. "Serves him right, that old fraud. He didn't want to let the President of Moldova's delegation in, then let him extend his sympathies!"

"Mister President." The lead pilot clapped Voronin on the shoulders. "Get ready."

The president stood up. He glanced at his advisors without parachutes and remembered something.

He pointed his thumb in their direction. "And with these ones – what'll we do?"

"Nothing," said the pilot, a young man, waving his hand. "Let them stay."

"Where?" The president didn't understand. "The plane can't fly back to Moldova without a pilot, can it?"

"Let them stay on the plane," the pilot explained. "That's my suggestion."

The president thought for a minute and decided that this was not a very good plan. Inhumane, somehow.

"Inhumane, somehow," he yelled to the pilot, who was already opening the hatch. "We're not animals, after all."

"Correct!" shouted the pilot. "We're people and, as distinct from animals, we have ideas, we can think."

"True!" affirmed the president.

"And so I was thinking and thinking, and this is what I thought up. If they manage to reach the plane right away … In other words, if they find two bodies, there'll be fewer questions. That's one. And if we take even one person to Italy for free, we'll destroy the whole business model. That's two. So, what'll it be?"

The president appraisingly glanced at his advisors, shrugged his shoulders and approached the open door. His hair was blown across his face by a mighty wind, and it was as if Voronin shed a dozen years. Right before he jumped, the pilot asked him one more time:

"So what'll we do with these two?

"Extend our sympathies."

34

SERAFIM, ENTANGLED IN THOUGHTS OF STELLA'S HAIR, RE-called the girl with sadness. He blamed life for the fact that things hadn't turned out as they might have. After all, Serafim had been in love with the librarian since first grade from the moment when, mesmerized by her slightly damp forehead, he sat down right on top of a pencil case. The years passed, they grew up, but the school desks had stayed the same. Stella had never let on that she liked him. "Maybe that's the reason I found a second love in my life – Italy," Serafim thought gloomily.

But it was hard to forget Stella. He recalled her lover, the head of the region, whose liaisons with Stella were the talk of the town; Serafim felt as if the invisible hand of the Archangel Gabriel was crushing his ribs. But he gradually, if begrudgingly, accepted his lot.

"What to do?" Serafim moaned quietly, so as not to wake Vasily. "You don't choose your fate. If she wasn't meant for me, she wasn't meant for me."

Serafim recalled, too, how he'd approached Stella for an Italian textbook he could use by himself, and how she was so cold to him, and how he tried to telepathically awake in her some feeling but was too shy to say to speak up and so he left, placing the blame on his own shoulders. And he thought that she hadn't given him another thought once he walked out the door, and that she'd immediately begun sprucing herself up in expectation of her lover's arrival.

What to do? In the life of every man, there's a woman who doesn't give a fiddle for him, and the life gets sucked out of him on her account, like sheep's cheese that's been taken out of the brine and thrown onto the display counter at the market ...

Serafim bit his lips and froze again. Then, with clear intentions, but carefully so as not to flip the boat, he stood up. Enough! He was a grown man. He had more to worry about than these boyhood diversions! Even if the eyes of his old flame were like dark grapes, and her chest rounded as a hill at the Dniester riverhead, and her body desired as a Christmas gift and supple as a young willow that grows through the frozen ground ... Enough! At the end of the day, he was no longer a boy. Serafim exhaled and peered ahead of him. It was already the tenth day of their expedition. The friends had been lucky with the weather. By all accounts it seemed that they weren't far from the shores of Italy. There was a lapping sound, and Serafim glanced around. A coastguard boat loomed suddenly before him. Serafim smiled and put his hands in the air.

"I greet you, valiant sons of Rome!" he shouted, in perfect Italian.

The coast guard laughed and Serafim relaxed. With a smile on his face, he immediately felt his head being plunged into the warm water of the welcoming sea. His legs shook as if from a blow, and Serafim was barely able to grab on to Vasily's collar. The coast guard, who had hit the submarine straight on with a hand grenade, sailed away without even bothering to check for survivors. Serafim held onto Vasily until morning, when they were picked up by Ukrainian sailors traveling to Odessa. From there, the friends were deported to Moldova.

"Welcome home, breadwinners!" the Moldovan customs inspector told them. "Don't tell me you're not carrying any money!"

35

IN FACT, THE ONLY REASON SERAFIM HAD GOTTEN HOLD of the book was because Stella, the librarian, was in love with him.

The region's librarian, Stella Zaporozhanu, had been in love with Serafim Botezatu since that day in the first grade when the strict village teacher sat them at the same desk. She stared the boy with the pained and pensive look on his face, his eye so hard to catch, and when she saw his thick eyebrows, she wondered if her own chest would be just as thick in ten years. Stella couldn't manage to grab his attention for nearly a half a year. She spent sleepless nights wondering where his eyes were always wandering.

And when she finally did catch the glance of her deskmate, her hopes were dashed, because she understood: only the most beautiful things in the world could catch his eye. His eye, reflected in her eye ... Since then, Stella'd had no peace of mind, and twenty years of life became hell. Especially after Serafim, upon turning fourteen, became obsessed with Italy and lost his interest in the world around him. And unlike her body, which blossomed and bloomed, Stella simply wilted inside.

"I dipped his photograph in wax. I stuck a pin into the hem of my dress. I brushed away his legs with my skirt, I secretly snipped off a lock of his hair to sink into my witch's brew at midnight and fan the flames of love. Is there a quack superstition I *haven't* tried?"

Stella's mother shook her head and advised her daughter to separate her heart from him. "He's not for you," she said, and she was right, because Serafim wasn't fit for

Stella. Nor was he fit for the woman his parents sought out to be his wife, though he dutifully lived with her. At his own wedding, Serafim sat with empty eyes and kept trying to understand: In Venice, did people enter a gondola with their left foot first or was it, after all, with the right foot?

After the wedding, Stella decided she'd never ever get married, cropped her hair and prepared herself for the monastery that was the regional library – which people visited even less frequently than an actual monastery. There she sat for years, buried in her dusty books, avoiding the wisdom of others and crying her heart out to the bats who had settled above the columns of the library's façade. The building was an old one, the former residence, perhaps, of local nobility.

"You don't get afraid here in the evenings?" The chairman of the collective farm stared at the young librarian.

And without waiting for an answer, he lay Stella on the table and quickly undressed her. Then he undressed himself, and climbed onto her hefty—in the end, they *had* grown thicker than Serafim's eyelashes—bosom. He mounted her sweaty legs, and her soft stomach, and her greasy underarms, and her slippery insides, and her hot flesh, and her skin, cool from sweat. Then he got up, wiped himself off without a word, and left. From then on the chairman came to Stella in the library every evening, and gradually she even learned to imagine that it was Serafim climbing atop her, and not another man. True, she still could not picture the face of her beloved. It had been ten years since she'd seen him, since she left the village for the regional center, for the library. Which is why, when the visitor came to see her, which in itself was a rarity, she didn't recognize him. It was only when the man quivered his eyelashes and said, "Do you have an Italian language textbook?" that she understood.

No matter how hard Stella tried to let Serafim know she was out of her mind for him, he remained deaf to her, and he left, leafing through the book he'd just borrowed from the library. The cover was missing, but all the other pages were there. Stella walked out to the doorway of the library but Serafim was already gone. She thought, how strangely designed is the heart of a man, who chases from dream to dream. Toward evening she gathered her things and left the regional center behind, closing the library and leaving the chairman forever to his yearnings for the flesh. After knocking on the door of her mother's house in Larga, Stella began to live on her native soil and await the return of Serafim from his trip to Italy. That he'd return, she did not doubt. Serafim wouldn't last an hour in Italy, Stella knew, because nobody would understand him, nor would he understand anything, either.

For Stella had slipped him a textbook – in Norwegian.

36

ITALIAN BORDER PATROL STAVES OFF IN-FILTRATION INTO THE COUNTRY BY AN ISLAMIC TERRORIST GROUP. On the Italian coast, a vessel was spotted and shot down by border police with a grenade launcher. On the vessel were what are presumed to be Islamic militants, intending to commit a terrorist act in Rome and its surroundings.

"This wasn't simply a coincidence," stated the press service for the Italian Carabinieri, "but the logical outcome of a long-planned operation, carried out by our best specialists. It has lasted approximately four years. We cannot reveal details for obvious reasons."

As Italy's law enforcement agencies have sparingly communicated, it is known that the terrorists tried to penetrate Italy with an amateur-built miniature submarine. The band of criminals consisted of thirty to fifty people, and all were destroyed when they refused to surrender their weapons and board the patrol boat of the Italian Coast Guard with their arms raised. The Carabinieri knew in advance that some of the fighters were native-born Europeans. Specifically, after the border guards deciphered one of the shouts, it became clear that the Islamists were speaking to each other in Norwegian. Prime Minister Berlusconi, commenting on the incident, pointed out the professionalism of Italy's elite units and reaffirmed Rome's intention of fulfilling her shared obligations regarding their American partner in Iraq.

"This international terrorist gang can't frighten us!" declared Berlusconi. "We are strong when we are united!"

In addition …

NEWS OF GREECE — 09.14.2005

BOAT WITH 75 MALNOURISHED MOLDOVAN IMMIGRANTS DISCOVERED IN MEDITERRANEAN SEA. Thirty more died of malnutrition and dehydration. The boat was discovered by a cargo vessel not far from the coast of Sicily. The injured victims were taken to Syracuse.

In the meantime, it has been established that the boat carrying the Moldovan immigrants had set out from Slovenia. The immigrants had each paid the smugglers four thousand dollars.

RUSSIAN INTERNATIONAL NEWS AGENCY — 06.12.2005

OSLO DENIES INFORMATION about Islamist training camps on Norwegian territory and expresses hope that an investigation of the incident off the Italian coast will be honest and unbiased. As the Minister of Interior Affairs commented …

BASA PRESS AGENCY — 06.12.2005

Newsflash! An airplane carrying the head of the Moldovan government has suffered a crash over the Italian Alps. Preliminary information shows no survivors. Details are still being confirmed. BASA-Press Agency is working non-stop to keep its subscribers up to date and informed on the conditions of the crash. Stay with us!"

INFOTAG AGENCY. 06.13.2005

Since the first broadcast of the program "Who Will Succeed President Voronin?" up to the current time—25 hours and 43 minutes in total, according to Infotag—our Internet news clip has been viewed by 150,000 visitors. Don't believe our competitors who claim to have more visitors than we do! Stay with us!

37

As it turned out, of course, Vasily and Serafim had no money at all. Nor did they have valuables, with the exception of a gold cross that Serafim used to calm his unbelieving heart. The customs guard tore the cross from the poor man's neck "for safekeeping" and locked the friends in a small prison at the border.

"Friends, this is my private, personal prison, so to speak," Mikhai Diorditse, the border guard, explained to them. "It's not a money-making racket, as my ill-wishers like to claim. It's solely in the spirit of private initiative, part of the general trend toward alignment with the European Union. That's all it is ... Sorry, where was I?"

"You were saying, this is your private, personal prison, so to speak," Vasily carefully reminded him.

"That's it! You got it!" remembered Mikhai. "Thus, you can be proud that you'll be the first Moldovans locked up in my private prison."

"And does that give us any special privileges?" inquired the practical Serafim.

"Sure," laughed Mikhai. "You can groan when they beat you, whimper when they put you to work, and eat what they feed you!"

Naturally, they weren't really the first prisoners here at all. That was just the guard's pretty turn of phrase. In the two-storey prison building with fat bars on the windows, an alarm system, and barbed wire along the perimeter, there were already close to a hundred people. Nearly half of these were gypsies from an encampment that had roamed the road from Soroki to Odessa to Nikolaevo and back, for more than 500 years. Even the Soviets had allowed it. But Diorditse the border guard, who was building up his cash reserves for the prison, stopped the gypsies during their usual crossing and, cursing a blue streak, put them in a close-by location.

"If you can pay Moldova back for crossing its national borders without documents and tariffs, I'll let you go," the border agent had said, clanking his keys. "Gyppos!"

The gypsies, of course, weren't about to work off their debt, since that would have contradicted their centuries-long way of life. In principle, life in prison on the government's dole was working out well for them, if only for one "but." While there were no expenses, per se, the inmates weren't fed.

"How will we survive, kind sir?" the head of the gypsy encampment asked Mikhai. "What use are we to you if we're dead? Gypsy stiffs don't pay ransom."

"Neither do live ones," said the border agent. "Figure it out for yourselves."

Figure it out they did. The gypsies dug a pond in the prison courtyard, which attracted flocks of pelicans on their migratory flights. The inmates caught the birds, salted and smoked them, and had what to eat for a year.

38

THE PRINCIPLE BEHIND CAPTAIN MIKHAI DIORDITSE'S private prison was simple. He'd gotten permission to open it with one condition: a ten percent cut of the ransom and the booty from the travelers would be marked straightaway for his boss, Major Dzhik Petrescu. Petrescu, in turn, was required to pass along a fifteen percent cut from what his subordinates, three captains of the border patrol, sent him. In four years Captain Diorditse made a name for himself and came into his own; his weight was now well over two hundred pounds, up from his previous one hundred and fifty. The question of whether his prison was a method for the illegal detention of citizens of Moldova and other countries didn't weigh on the captain's conscience. After all, a private prison was an undertaking in the spirit of entrepreneurial initiative, an attitude widely hailed in Moldova.

"I'm happy for anything that brings us closer to Europe," President Voronin, who recently died tragically when his plane crashed into the mountains, used to say.

And so Diorditse did what he could. Weren't there private prisons in Europe? Customs posts? In the final reckoning, thought Mikhai, what's the most important principle to the European way of thinking? To raise capital and accumulate assets! And when there are assets, then they get put to good use, because money gets put into circulation. So Diorditse raised capital, and circulated it.

From time to time Mikhai, a captain in the customs office, would reflect sadly that the moribund Moldovan parliament didn't offer much stimulus for the creation of

The Good Life Elsewhere

small private armies. Maybe not armies, per se, but well-armed militias, consisting of fifty or so people. Mikhai was relaxing after his shift and daydreaming in good humor. This militia would serve both him and Moldova. They could collect tariffs. They'd be of great use to him, Mikhai Diorditse, and who is it that makes up the country if not people like him, Mikhai Diorditse? Of course, there was Major Dzhik Petrescu, and Colonel Afanasy Vier, and others, too …

Occasionally Mikhai contemplated speaking with his higher-ups and seeking permission to print his own money. Well, why not? It would be convenient. You print your own money and then … Dreaming about this, the captain became excited, got out of bed and walked barefoot out into the prison yard. The gypsies had long been lying in wait, snares in hand, ready for the flock of pelicans who alighted on the water of the manmade pond every spring like clockwork.

"Hey Footlose," the captain cheerily shouted to one of the gypsies, who was sitting off to the side. "What are you so down about? As soon as you pay, you can walk away."

"How many times do I have to repeat myself?" the gray-haired, bearded gypsy shouted, waving his fist in the air. "I'm not a gypsy. And I'm not Footloose! I'm an actor from the city of Balti, my last name is Volontir, Mikhai's what they call me. I look like a gypsy because that's how they made me up on the bus that was taking our troop to Odessa for a performance. For the life of me I can't understand why you took me off that bus and why you're arbitrarily holding me here. It's been four years!"

The border guard scratched his shoulder. "You're a real fruit loop, Footloose." He sounded surprised.

Then he turned around and sat down by the water. Five minutes later, a frog swam up to the surface. The border guard carefully extracted an antediluvian but serviceable pistol from his chest holster. He took aim and fired. The frog scrambled off. Footloose clutched at his heart and began to curse Diorditse. Volontir, the actor, had never gotten used to the captain's favorite pastime. The border guard Mikhai had a great big belly laugh, after which he turned around to the prisoner and shot him in the leg.

"Footloose, you're trying my patience," he said, taking a deep breath. "Thank you very much, don't spoil my fun anymore with your dirty insults, which a well brought up person wouldn't dare speak out loud!"

"How many times do I have to tell you," the gypsy began to howl, grabbing his leg, "My name—"

The border guard shot the prisoner's other leg.

"—is Footloose," finished Volontir. "I am a gypsy, and my name is Footloose."

"One more time."

"Foot—," howled Volontir, "—loose!"

Diorditse smiled and tucked his pistol back into the holster. Then he remembered why he'd come outside. To the people, as they say.

"Hey, you," Diorditse called to the new prisoner, Vasily Lungu, who'd been locked up for crossing the border without a passport but, even more serious, without money. "You're a craftsman. A real man of the people, as they say. Get over here."

Vasily unhurriedly walked on over. Serafim, who'd been digging planting rows in the land, straightened up and rubbed his back.

"You best keep working. This ain't Soviet Land anymore, where an idiot like you did nothing all day but guzzle vodka. Labor, as it's written in the Gospels. And you, Mister Craftsman, tell me one thing."

"I'm all ears, Captain, Sir," Vasily answered gloomily. He was thirsting for freedom, and after three months in prison he was emaciated. His Italian dream had been completely abandoned.

"Now tell me," the border guard winked slyly, "would I be able to print my own money here? Don't get any wrong ideas about me. Mind your own business. I'm more interested in the technical aspects, so to say."

"Money?" asked Vasily. Hard as a copper penny, he said, "Of course. You can make real money, Captain, Sir."

"From precious metals?" the border guard asked soberly. "Can we make do without?"

"What do you mean?"

"You know," said the border guard dreamily. "Can we print money without spending any on it?"

Serafim, who'd been eavesdropping on the conversation, walked up and added his two cents. He was staking everything on this next moment.

"Now, you see," he said quickly, hoping that the border guard wouldn't have time to get angry and bring his Mauser into the conversation. (He'd confiscated the gun from real contrabandists.) "The task which you put before Vasily is not entirely a technical question. And in our partnership, everything that's not technical is taken care of by me. I can tell you that the operation you've thought up is completely realizable. You can absolutely, without a hitch, introduce currency of private provenance into circulation in the region, and you won't have to spend almost anything to do it."

"Huh?" Mikhai Diorditse's jaw dropped. He was a graduate of the Academy of Economics.

"You can print a crapload of cash without spending a fartin' dime on it!!" Serafim explained.

"That's more like it." Diorditse scratched his nose with the barrel of his Mauser. "Now go on. But make sure my nose stays clean."

"Places along the border are dangerous," said Serafim. "Full of all kinds of bandits, tricksters, outlaws. And all of them have a hankering for the wallet of the traveler.

Especially when he's a worker who's returning home from Italy or Russia with some cash. Right?"

"Right," said Diorditse, who still didn't understand a thing. "And?"

"And we have his best interests in mind!" Serafim grandly raised a finger to the air. "Rather, you do. Print your own money, and then explain that it's worthless and good for nothing. And upon their entry, you'll confiscate all their euros and dollars and rubles, and replace them with your own currency."

"But won't the currency be worthless and good for nothing?" the captain pointed out.

"Right," Serafim said hastily. "Which means, nobody's fingers will itch for it. And the workers will bring their earnings home, safely and untouched. And all thanks to whom? Thanks to you, a genius of financial thinking, the father of the Moldovan working people, Captain of the Border Guards Diorditse."

"But when they get home, won't they need to exchange our currency for real, normal money?" the captain pointed out.

"Well, why?" Serafim shrugged his shoulders. "Either way they'll drink it all away. Better to set up a small store in every village where people can buy the basics, but using only your currency. And you'll set the prices where you want them."

"And where do I want them?"

"For example, a can of juice would cost ten euros," suggested Serafim.

"Why so expensive?" The captain, like all Moldovans, loved to bargain.

"Let them go try to find a cheaper price, when they've got no money!" concluded Serafim triumphantly.

The captain looked at the prisoner sadly.

"So it's like this," he said. "They won't let me do this across the whole country, but they'll allow it in the border region. As an experiment, let's say. This craftsman here will print money, using some junk materials. And don't ever lose sight of the fact that you're here by my side forever and a day…"

"Yes," said Serafim in a whisper.

"I would shoot you to get rid of the competition, but I won't remember everything you just said," admitted the border guard. "So you'll be my bookkeeper."

Serafim nodded obediently and he and Vasily walked back arm in arm to the furrowed land. The sky suddenly darkened and snow-white pelicans rushed down upon the lake. The gypsies readied their snares. A frog poked its head out of the water.

Captain Diorditse took aim.

39

"Quicker!" Serafim was hurrying. "For the sake of Italy, our holy dream, I'm asking you! I'm begging you! Quicker!"

Serafim heard a cry at his back and in a huff of rage he pulled Vasily into the ravine. Their pursuers—Diorditse's most skilled guards with their Dobermans—were getting closer. The friends had lost nearly all their strength after a year in jail, thanks to the impossible work and meager rations. Now they were escaping; they looked like tubercular cows. But for the friends, there was no way out except to run. They both understood that Captain Diorditse would never let them go. It was because of Serafim's brains and Vasily's hands that the border guard was earning such huge piles of cash. After getting leave to go work in the cornfields, the pair took off running.

"We won't get away," Vasily exhaled, breaking into a wheeze. "We're not gonna make it. Goodbye, my brother."

"What are you talking about? You can't give up!" Serafim pleaded. "What about Italy? Hold on! We'll make our escape, catch our breath somewhere, and then we'll make for Italy. And we'll get there! I give my word, we'll get there. I know you don't believe ... "

"I believe," answered Vasily. "I believe ... that *you'll* get there. When you talk about Italy, I can see the truth looming in your eyes. If you don't make it, it means there's no God, and no truth, either."

"Can you forgive me for dragging you into all this mess?" Serafim begged.

"Forget about it," said Vasily, and waved his hand listlessly. "Fate is fate. What I want to know is, does it exist? Italy, I mean?"

"Yes, yes, believe me. And we'll be there together. Listen to me. Listen! We're going to cross this ravine and throw ourselves into the little river. The current will carry us. We'll make it out of here, brother!"

"I won't survive ... "

Serafim stood up again, lifted Vasily onto his back and broke into a run. "Forget about that! We're getting out of here. We have to get out of here."

The security guards crowded together at the edge of the hill and silently watched Serafim, with Vasily on his back, hop his way across small rivulets as he made for the river, which lay directly beyond the hill. He ran unabashedly, like a woman who's not embarrassed to show a strange man her underarm.

"They'll get away," said Footloose, who'd been promoted to head of security. "We won't catch them. The dogs, either. We're supposed to take 'em alive."

"I'll aim for the leg," said the best sharpshooter among them. "Here goes ... "

Serafim ran and ran, like in a dream where you expend titanic effort but nothing ever changes. As if in slow motion, the water splashed high when his legs came crashing down. The golden leaves of the Moldovan autumn sank into the mud; it was impossible to tell where the shore ended and the river began. The icy fog provided cover for the path to the river and Serafim greedily sucked the cold air into his hot mouth. As he sank in up to his belt, he had decided he was a goner when the river's waters whirled and twirled and carried him and Vasily away. They'd broken clear.

Using his left hand as an oar, Serafim grabbed Vasily with his right and said what he hadn't managed to say in the ravine. Vasily smiled.

"We're gonna make it to Italy. Everything'll change," said Serafim. "There'll be no more Moldovan mud in our lives, no more terrible poverty hanging over our heads like a scab on a bald tramp's noggin. No more of this interminable, hellish work, which makes you want to howl louder than a dog on the doorstep of a penny-pinching priest."

The noise of the chase dissipated into silence, and the warm water of the river quietly lapped against the faces of the friends; the willow branches hung lower along the banks.

"Museums, culture, even the air there shines with light. The sky glitters with rays of sunshine, and the earth itself blossoms with unfading, fragrant flowers and beautifully blooming eternal trees that yield blessed fruits," Serafim went on, dreamily.

And to the friends, it seemed that this fragrant smell was already hovering above them and above the Prut, that ancient Moldovan River.

Serafim went on: "And Italians aren't as sneaky, rude, mean and lazy as we Moldovans are. They aren't such knuckledragging knuckleheads. They even dress differently. Their clothes are just like their country. Happy and festive! The people are beautiful. They all sing Italy's praises, because there's what to sing about. Not like Moldova, which asks you for love, but is less of a motherland than a *step*-motherland!"

Serafim went on for a long time about this fairytale land of Italy, and the water of the river seconded his opinion in a whisper. The moon shone in the black sky and the friends were no longer afraid. They were no longer afraid of the two hundred pound catfish that, it was rumored, had been grabbing people by the legs in the past two years and dragging them down to the riverbed of the Prut. They weren't afraid of snakes that could climb into the very sky itself by the light of the moon and fall onto the head of a person who, laying down to sleep, hadn't made a sign of the cross above his head with the proper two fingers. The men floated in the very center of the river, and the whirlpools, upon seeing them, covered them with their black, swirling ink. The gnarled tree branches floating in the river became soft, like the hair of a drowned woman. The fish leapt out of the water like mischievous dolphins, in order to say hello to Serafim and Vasily. From the lake that lay close by, a chorus of frogs reached their ears. And above the mellow, low din, the tinkling of bells rose up to the reaches of the universe, along with the footfalls of a flock of sheep, wandering somewhere along the well-worn pasturelands and bringing with them their bells. And in Serafim's heart for the first time there began to shine the emptiness of the impending separation from his unbeloved homeland, but his homeland nonetheless ...

Vasily, however, no longer had a heart, since it had been torn asunder by a guard's bullet.

40

Up to his knees in water, Serafim spent a few minutes looking at the pale face of his friend one last time, then began sending Vasily off for a final float. He wrapped Lungu's hands in a dead grip around his admiral's cap. Serafim was sorry he didn't have a rifle for a final salute but he had to content himself with a speech.

"My dear friend," Serafim began nervously. He was holding Vasily tightly, so as not to let the water carry him off too soon. "At this difficult moment of parting ... No, that's too official-sounding ... I'm sorry, Vasily... Hmm ... On his best days, the dearly departed ... No, that's not right ... The deceased ..."

His knees were in sharp pain from standing in the cold water. Serafim thought for a minute, sliced his hand through the air and started over:

"I have a dream. If God does exist, after all, I hope that sooner or later He gathers us all together. The humble and the destitute, the dejected and the wretched. That He gathers your wife, Maria, you, me, Old Man Tudor from our village of Larga and another three million Moldovans, and possibly a few gypsies, and gives us all a seat at His right hand. So that we can look at each other and forget the pain we inflicted on our loved ones, and so we can begin to live in heaven, like in Italy. And so that, in the Italian afterlife, we receive everything we never had in our lifetime in Moldova ... "

Having finished, Serafim cocked his ears. The river was whirling with a disapproving rush. Even the broken tree around the nearest bend was creaking somehow discontentedly. Really, it wasn't much of a parting speech, more of a conference talk, thought Serafim unhappily. He crossed himself, then sighed. "I'm sorry, Vasily, that even this last version was so ... so ... unfit. I'll come up with something else right away... "

Serafim spent the entire day trying to come up with a speech, until even the dead man could take it no longer and grew angry.

"Hey, Serafim, quit trying to catch a tiger by the tail! Be a man! One, two, say goodbye to your friend, you were a reliable comrade and a faithful husband, three, four, now send his body off to the water."

Guiltily shaking his head, that's just what Serafim did. And he cried, watching Vasily's corpse disappear around the bend; he cried all the way home to Larga, where he arrived the following evening, toward twilight, which hung so darkly beneath the celestial dome that a torch could be seen burning on the outskirts of town. As he approached, Serafim looked at the burning column. It was a giant pillar, some three meters high. All ablaze, it crackled, showering sparks and hot grease, as well as dirty slanders and dying curses.

The villagers were grandly setting fire to Old Man Tudor.

41

For Old Man Tudor, the loss of the bicycle Vasily and Serafim had "borrowed" for its pedals was a heavy blow. It was too difficult for Tudor to reach the fields on foot, which were some six miles from his house. His workday extended by four hours and Old Man Tudor, sweating his guts out sixteen hours a day, understood that this was the end.

The first two months after his bicycle disappeared, all Old Man Tudor could do was pace his yard like a freshly-widowed swan, and lament.

"Where could it have gotten to? Where?" Tudor would ask at a loss. "It's too bad Serafim's gone off somewhere. That fellow's got eyes sharper than a falcon. He would have helped me find my bicycle. I must have put the damned contraption somewhere, and in my old age, I can't remember where."

The leaves on the calendar flew off the wall like kernels of corn during husking. Meanwhile, the bicycle was still missing. Winter spread its white bedsheets across the hilly breast of Moldova, but the bicycle never showed. Spring managed to pull off the soiled, snowy blanket, but the bicycle hadn't bicycled on back. Finally, summer came and healed the dirty puddles, like open wounds, in the village roads. And still, no bicycle.

In the fall Old Man Tudor found out the truth, which his fellow villagers had carefully hidden from the old man out of pity.

"Serafim took Tudor's bike to use for the submarine he

and Vasily swam off in," Tudor overheard somebody say at a christening. "Just don't tell the old man, else he's liable to lose his mind. He loved Serafim like a son." Suddenly, everything was clear.

The next day, Old Man Tudor arrived at church, pushed Father Paisii from the pulpit, raised his hand and asked for the floor.

"Good Moldovans," he began, " I greatly wish to tell you my thoughts about Italy. Listen, and remember well: Italy ... DOES NOT EXIST."

The church broke into the usual collective groan. From somewhere the shriek of a baby could be heard. But Uncle Tudor was inexorable.

"Italy is an old wives' tale, and pretty soon they'll have you chasing your tail, while they've got your four thousand euros. Italy doesn't exist. When the priest took you on that holy crusade to Italy, he fooled you. There's no such thing as heaven! There's no blessed earth where you get honey from the tap instead of water, where people breed big fat carp fish in their bathtubs, and where the housemaids get paid a thousand euros a month. None of that exists!"

The congregation looked at him in terror. Just like Martin Luther, Tudor banged his fists on the pulpit and made an appeal.

"Open your eyes, people! They're leading you by the nose with their fairy tales about Italy. You leave behind the place where your ancestors settled, you discard your homeland in order to travel to God knows where and do who knows what. And your flocks grow sparse, your earth wastes away, your women and children whither without you!"

"Aww, come on, everything wastes away even when we're here!" a voice from behind the icon wall timidly objected. "Boy, it sure does collapse and waste away!"

"And it's all because you leave this place, quit your inheritance, and don't maintain order in your homes!" howled Tudor. "They feed you these cock and bull stories about some Italian paradise. They distract you from your pain, from what really needs to be fixed. People, open your eyes. Italy doesn't exist!"

The people listened, unable to believe their ears. One person cried; another crossed himself. Tudor went on.

"Understand, you wretched of the earth, we should strive to improve what we can. Here. Right here, in Moldova. We can clean our own houses; fix our own roads. We can trim our own shrubs and work the fields. We can stop gossiping, drinking and loafing. We can become kinder, more patient, more tender with each other. We can stop ripping pages out of library books and spitting on a cleanly swept floor. Quit deceiving. Start living honest lives. Italy—the real Italy—is in us ourselves!"

The crowd grew loud with threats. Unfriendly hands stretched out toward Old Man Tudor. With a deep breath, he managed to say a few last words:

"Henceforth, I will be the village priest. And I declare that belief in Italy is heresy! Because the real Italy is located within each one of us. And from now on, that's what we believe in. Let me g—"

42

*OLD MAN TUDOR, THE HERETIC FROM THE VILLAGE OF LARGA,
was the cause of the Second Holy Crusade to Italy. Father
Paisii, our leader, came from the same village. It was said
that only Larga, the birthplace of our true spiritual father,
could also be the birthplace of an antichrist such as Old Man
Tudor. It was said also that even in all his diabolical stubbornness and malice, Old Man Tudor was fulfilling a role
ordained for him by God. For it was precisely Tudor's heresy
which awoke our beloved village priest Paisii from his spiritual slumber. After the unfortunate First Crusade, Father
Paisii was guilty of the sin of despair, and was nearly ready to
lay down his arms – those same arms which bore the miracle-
working crucifix of the true Moldovan Orthodox faith.*

*After appearing in church one day, Tudor stood at the
pulpit and prophesized his true heresy. By all accounts, he
declared Italy does not exist, it was all fairy tales. He delivered various other ungodly heresies, from which the hearts of
the true Christians blazed up in anger. And they joined their
numbers, and they tied up Old Man Tudor, and they stood
him before an Orthodox tribunal, in which I took part – I,
the former village teacher, now the Chronicler of the First
and Second Holy Crusades to Italy. And I recorded some of
the questions put to Tudor, who was chained to an enormous
pillar for his refusal to believe in the one true God and in
Italy. And they beat him without mercy, torturing him also
with their words.*

*In accordance with our duties, the prosecutor demanded
Tudor take an oath with one hand resting on the Gospels,
as per court protocol. This was in order that he should vow*

to tell the truth in reply to each question they asked him. And the one called Tudor answered saying: "I know not what you will ask me. It is possible you will ask me that which I will not tell you." We said to him, "Swear to speak the full truth when they will ask you concerning your faith and what you are aware of." Again he answered that as for what he is aware of, he will gladly swear. But as for what he is not aware of, he claimed the right not to answer the tribunal. In response to this, Father Paisii ordered for boiling water to be poured down Tudor's throat. He asked where Tudor learned his heretical ideas about the nonexistence of Italy as earthly paradise. And Tudor, despite his torture, spoke evil things, declaring that God does not exist, nor Italy, and offending the court in every possible way. And we, having considered his delusions, took the difficult decision to save the heretic's soul by destroying his earthly body.

Even as he was set on fire, he delivered an heretical speech wherein he claimed that Italy is not paradise but an inner state of existence inside each one of us, which claim was re- jected by Father Paisii. Further, Tudor said, one can reach that state of existence without paying four thousand euros, without clergy and without Holy Crusades. We spat and crossed ourselves upon hearing these abominations, and sum- moned Satan to burn the wretched Tudor verily with speed.

And the heart of the burned one, and his black ashes, we tossed into the waters of the Dniepr River, so that even the memory of Old Man Tudor the heretic would be washed away.

And afterwards Father Paisii, as if waking from a dream, ordered the people to gather for a Second Holy Crusade to Italy.

And unto each one was promised:
the forgiveness of sins;
a place in Heaven upon their death;
the full property of the heretics, who do not believe in the true Moldovan Orthodox God and Italy;

and also the spoils of the cities and towns;
guaranteed employment in Italy;
and an Italian residency permit.

And on the morning of the Second Crusade one hundred and ninety thousand people gathered in Larga, of whom one hundred thousand were children. And having mounted his horse, Father Paisii rode at the head. And as the multitude moved across Moldova, the numbers of the Holy Army increased.

And the children, being warriors for Christ, were exceedingly joyful and blessed with pure hearts, and strong in their intentions to make the pilgrimage to Italy, the land promised to every faithful Moldovan. And they joined in circles and sang songs, and praised Father Paisii and Italy, and their beloved parents, whom they would see again in Italy. And though there were many teenage boys and girls among these children, Father Paisii permitted them to move in one column, unafraid of sin, saying:

"What is pure at heart cannot be foul in the flesh. And even if a lad sins with a lass, for their participation in our pious activities I guarantee these young ones, by my oath, forgiveness of this mild sin."

And Father Paisii became even more popular among the youth. And very soon in many regions of Moldova, young men and women became apostles. They drew close to them throngs of likeminded people and led them, with banners and crosses, and with majestic song, to the miracle-working Father Paisii. And when an onlooker asked these young men and women whither they traveled, he received the same answer:

"To Italy. To our parents."

One year before the Second Holy Crusade many Moldovans had arrived to Italy in roundabout ways and were laboring there, but could not bring their children. The children shot up like weeds but did not forget their parents. And when Father Paisii promised to bring them to Italy, not through *the servant's entrance but through the main gates, they re-joiced and followed after him. And nobody could restrain the children from this undertaking, nor were there those who wanted to.*

Verily, the people were expecting a miracle. Once the Italian rulers beheld them, so said the people, two hundred thousand children, yearning for the embrace of their mothers and fathers, then the heart of Rome would surely expand and grant every Moldovan the right to work in Italy without a visa and to bring with him whichever of his loved ones he desired. And only the children, free of turpitude, could give the Moldovan people something to replace the Holy Sepulchre; only they could grant us our innermost dreams.

Only the children could deliver us the blessed land of Italy.

43

MEANWHILE, AS FATHER PAISII'S TWO HUNDRED THOUSAND children were marching toward Italy in one column, with their gonfalons, their swords and faith in their hearts; as thousands of Moldovans paid for the privilege of being secreted into Moldova in hidden automobile compartments, risking capture and forcible return to Moldova; while the earth carried forward the Moldovans and their Italy ...

... Vasily Lungu had found peace, and without hindrance or obstacle was floating with the river's tide toward the Black Sea. From there he began his doleful water voyage, carried by the waves of the sea toward Italy, where his dead body was aiming. Along the way, Vasily was greatly changed. His hair had grown by several meters during the course of his journey and now it ranged across the face of the drowned man like the tentacles of a strange sea creature. His fingernails had stratified into twenty layers, so that Vasily's hands looked like the fins of a mythical merman. The Southern European's skin, brown and tightly wound across his cheekbones, had whitened, like the finest linen, and stretched, so that Vasily's face took on the placid look that one loses at birth. His nostrils fluttered with the rhythms of the water which filled it, and his body slackened. And finally, Vasily was at rest, after these thirty-five years of his life. His face relaxed, and Vasily forgot how he'd looked in his lifetime. Little fish nibbled at his arms; crabs pierced his spine.

At the Romanian coast, below Constanta, he encountered the Brazilian water goddess Yamanja and offered her his passionate caresses, as heated as Moldovan despair. Near Slanica, he collided with a sculpture of Pallas that had fallen off the nose of an ancient Greek ship, and now made its home in the sea. Near Mangalia, Vasily saw a giant squid which the Irish monk Peter the Wise had written about in the Twelfth Century; he was surprised at how accurately the man had described this sea monster. Then Vasily floated out from the Black Sea into the Adriatic. He was surprised yet again by how the two seas fit into each other, like Russian nesting dolls.

Vasily floated, gradually turning into something amorphous, into a jelly-like lump swaying in the beating heart of the ocean, and he was happy as never before. The ocean was an enormous womb, and he – a baby.

"That's it, my true homeland," the drowned man thought to himself, "the ocean!"

And so, joyfully anticipating his encounter with the ocean, the heart of which beat ever stronger inside him, Vasily finally left behind the warm Adriatic Sea and exited, through the Pillars of Hercules, into the ocean. And the colossal enormity of it surprised Vasily, just as shouts of "Land!" had surprised Columbus. The waves broke in their rage against the columns, seagulls joyfully greeted Vasily, and the seals barked. They played atop the columns with the disk we call the sun, instead of with a ball. Their barking merged with the din of the ocean, and gave rise to tears of pure happiness in the frayed heart of Vasily. And he, or rather, that tiny part of him which remained, broke free into the open water. And the strongest and largest wave encompassed Vasily, and the pathetic remains of his body dissipated into the foam. And they spun, each particle a tiny planet in orbit.

Vasily Lungu, citizen of the ocean, returned home forever.

44

In May, the fields of Romanian Moldova were covered in flowers as pale as the countenances of the local residents. Last year's haystacks jutted out of the landscape here and there, but nobody had any use for them. Nor would they. Winter in Moldova, of course, isn't the same as winter beyond the Prut River, but there, in the land that had once been Moldova but was now called Romania, where Stefan the Great had reigned four hundred years ago – all the livestock had perished. The Romanians blamed it on the Moldovan sorcerers whom Father Paisii brought to their land three years prior. Officially, Bucharest did not confirm these rumors, but neither did they deny them. The Romanian president had long ago dreamed of getting rid of the troublesome ad hoc settlement that came to be known as Eurograd. He had even planned on meeting with Father Paisii, in order to dot all his i's and cross his t's. But the priest, who'd already received the invitation from President Basescu, had something else on his mind that day.

"Just take a look. What a beautiful maiden!" they shouted at his back. "I'd like to ride a mare like that."

The jesters kept up the banter. "Now let's give her … a wide berth."

Father Paisii hunched up his shoulders, which made him look completely pathetic and shriveled. He tossed his hood high upon his head and began galloping quicker. From behind, the longhaired, slender-bodied priest looked an awful lot like a girl. Paisii stole a glance at his watch and darted toward the tent city. He had to hurry.

In just a few minutes in Eurograd there'd be the usual delivery of wine cisterns. Then the ubiquitous bingeing would begin. It would end, as a rule, with rape and pillage. And then they wouldn't let him through. Paisii knew that they'd lift up his cassock, and then the people would see that it was he, the priest. The threat of sexual assault which loomed, whether he was actually a woman or not, would be mere child's play compared to what would happen if they discovered that it was *him* trying to escape.

"They'll burn me like that miserable Tudor," Paisii whispered grievously and bit his lips. "Oh, cruel mob. I never asked for a wretch's death."

The mob was savage, Paisii well knew, and he understood that if they caught him, he couldn't count on mercy. Children are the cruelest of humans, after all, and out of the hundred and ten thousand residents of Eurograd, one hundred and eight thousand of them were teenagers, ranging from twelve to eighteen years old. The crimes they committed in the city every single minute were agonizing in their cruelty and savageness. Eurograd, Paisii realized with grief, was a focal point of evil. A true Babylon of our day. Nero's Rome, transplanted into Romania in 2005 by the caprice of the Devil. And he, Paisii, shouldered all the blame.

Everything had started out so well.

45

GOD, *HAVING ARRANGED EVERYTHING FOR US TO REACH BLESSED Italy, our destination, changed His mind. The insight and intentions of Providence destroyed us for our sins. Nonetheless, I shall describe all the events in the order they occurred. My labor as Chronicler of the Holy Crusade of Father Paisii will serve as evidence of the sincerity of my words. In the secular world, I was the schoolteacher in a village called Larga in a country known as Moldova. This aided me in becoming a Chronicler.*

Gathering together roughly two hundred thousand people, more than three quarters of whom were children, Father Paisii undertook a crusade to Italy, a land considered holy by all Moldovans. This Promised Land now languished under the legs of the impious Italians, Paisii said, and we were to liberate it and populate Italy with true Orthodox believers. But the First Holy Crusade—the chronicle of which I laudably and painstakingly recorded—did not come to completion. We were scattered as the Egyptians were scattered by Divine Providence. Father Paisii explained this was because we, the Moldovans of a certain age, proved unworthy of the lot God intended for us. And because of the absence of pure thoughts in the army of the Holy Crusade, the effort was destroyed. Therefore, in the Second Crusade, Paisii commanded that only children should participate. Only they, clean of soul and mind, could save Italy from the impure Italians and open the door of the divine world to us, the Moldovans.

The first three months we spent idly, following after Father Paisii across all of Moldova, completing the Crucession and saying prayers, bringing joy to the local population with our hymns in glory of Italy and God, and stocking up on victuals, sometimes without the consent of the people who supplied them. Around the time of the third month, signs of corruption appeared in Father Paisii's army: boys and girls were copulating with such vigor that even Father Paisii, who had already forgiven his flock for these sins, called upon them to be more restrained and to remember the ultimate goal of our undertaking.

When we had journeyed for four months, finally, we crossed the River Prut. Nothing could stop us, neither the Romanian border guards, nor the water, which on that day was abnormally quiet and calm and not a barrier. In this we saw that our undertaking was of God and we rejoiced.

And at the outskirts of the city Iassi we were surrounded by the army and they compelled us to halt, but Father Paisii called for negotiations. And the Romanian president said he was unable to let our army cross over his country, but his feelings of Romanian brotherhood would not allow him to bomb and shoot at us. Especially since all of Romania was very touched by the genuine yearning of the youth of Moldova toward Europe. Father Paisii and President Basescu assessed the situation and reached the following conclusion: Romania committed to building us a tent city with several buildings made of stone. And to contribute construction materials, with which we ourselves would be responsible for building the city. And Romania also pledged to become an advocate for Moldova in the European Parliament and to intercede for the two hundred thousand Moldovan children, so they might be allowed into Italy, and that no obstacles be put in their way. But the miserable Italians objected, and the Romanian efforts saw no success.

And we named the city Eurograd, in honor of Europe and European integration. And we came to live there, waiting for a decision on our fate from the European Parliament. But God inflicted madness upon us, and the Moldovan children began to pervert Eurograd into a semblance of their own

The Good Life Elsewhere

country, which they had abandoned. They shook the dust of their homeland off their feet.

In Eurograd, corruption, theft, violence and lawlessness multiplied furiously, like lilac in the groves along the banks of the Dniester. One could not take a step in the city without paying a bribe. Evenings, the young cross-bearers would commit violence against each other, brawls and knife-fights flashed up in the city. The streets of Eurograd turned into a rubbish heap that pigs would not shy away from. The women sold themselves for food, the stronger youths took everything by force, and the weaker ones abased themselves, attempting at least to inflict pain upon those weaker still than themselves. Nobody utilized the sewer system that had been dug by the Romanians. People answered nature's call directly in the streets, and into the streets they threw their garbage and poured out their slops. The public bathhouse was burned to the ground. Tuberculosis appeared. Many residents were lice-ridden. Two universities that had been opened for purposes of self-improvement in anticipation of Italy were looted. But there was not only destruction in Eurograd. There was also creation.

They built four hundred public houses in three years in the city, where spirits were sold by the glass and by the bottle, for a swallow and for a barrel. The crowds of children brazenly ignored Father Paisii's words. Street gangs and clans, criminal authorities and swindlers were everywhere.

And our dream of becoming pure, of being worthy of Italy, perished.

And the entire world was astonished by our wretchedness when they looked upon our city. And Italy, in light of all this, forbade us straightaway from crossing over into its land. And when the residents of Eurograd, hearing this, attempted to continue their Holy Crusade, Italy's whips and cudgels turned them back. And they continued to decay and die.

Ipso facto, Eurograd became Moldova.

46

PAISII'S THOUGHTS TURNED TO CURRENT EVENTS. HE teared up and lifted himself onto his elbows. The priest was lying on the ground at the edge of the tent city's border. The roar of trucks reached him from afar and floodlights flickered near the tents. The lights were Eurograd's evening illumination system, installed by the Romanians, who surrounded the city with troops. They didn't allow anyone to leave the city, but they did let in lines of vehicles carrying food, alcohol, and other goods. Right now they were supposed to be hauling in three cisterns of port wine.

"They've brought sweet wine," somebody standing near the cisterns laughed. "For dessert!"

Teenagers walked away from the cisterns clanging their full buckets. Many of them were drinking right at the cistern, and fell down drunk on the spot. The Romanian merchants kicked them disdainfully, all the while keeping an eye on their accounts. One of the boys didn't have enough money so he brought over his ten-year-old sister. The wine merchant suspiciously wrinkled his face, poured out a potful of poison and, as the young man guzzled it down, whisked the girl away to the cab of his vehicle. An hour later, he shoved her out of the car, bruised and crying, and said something to the brother. The brother, already good and drunk, mumbled a response, after which the merchant poured him a bucket of wine. He picked up the girl—who was so afraid of being beaten and raped that she couldn't even speak—and locked her in the car. "He's going to take her away," realized Paisii. "He bought her, now he's taking her away." But Paisii took himself in hand and turned away.

Paisii waited until all the wine had been poured out into smaller buckets and brought into the city center. Toward night, creeping quietly along the ground, he climbed onto a truck and slipped into an empty wine cistern. Pulling a gas mask over his face, he got down on his haunches and nearly burst out sobbing with relief. In sum, the three-year attempt at controlling uncontrollable teenagers—*Moldovan* teenagers, to boot—had turned Paisii into a sentimental crybaby.

"You've broken free!" Paisii whispered to himself. "You've broken free! Now, if only I could go home and sleep this off!"

The vehicle drove off and the priest fell asleep. Due to the lack of oxygen, his dreams were surprisingly vivid. At first his runaway wife, Angela, shamelessly waved her thigh from somewhere deep in the night. Paisii ran after her leg, grabbed it and began squeezing it. Then, without any ceremony, he threw the strumpet to the ground and had his way with her. And then the priest looked around and saw the girl who'd been purchased by the wine merchant. The merchant was nowhere in sight. Paisii stole up on the little girl, clamped her mouth shut, threw her to the ground and had his way with her, just like his wife. Then all of a sudden, from deep in the night, the wine seller appeared. He forced Paisii to put on his gasmask, and then the merchant had his way with him, just as the priest had done to his wife.

The light streaming into the cistern through the open cover roused Paisii from his sleep. He was covered in sweat. He made sure nobody was looking, then he took off his gasmask and climbed out for a breath of fresh air. It was sweeter than wine. With an open cistern the car drove on, one of a column of vehicles approaching a border of sorts. With a squint, Paisii read the road sign. He couldn't believe his eyes, so he read it again.

3 MILES TO ITALIAN BORDER

The priest rubbed his eyes. He was nearly sure the wine was causing him to hallucinate. Then he recalled overhearing talk in Eurograd about wine-producing firms in Italy where Moldovans held jobs under the table. They made wine that was cheap, sweet and strong. Then they forged documents to make the wine appear to be from Moldova and brought it to sell in Russia. "They must be selling it in Eurograd, too," realized Paisii, and he fell deep in thought. At that moment he looked very much like a tank soldier, leaning his torso out of the hatch of his combat vehicle. Father Paisii was the soldier, the cistern was his tank, and here he was, Father Paisii, overtaking the last three miles of his Ten Years' War.

Paisii dusted off his lapels and breathed in a chestful of sky from approaching Italy.

47

THE AIRPLANE MADE A STEEP TURN AND BEGAN TO CLIMB. The Croatian Air Force combat craft, an old crop duster, could climb for half an hour and still barely be off the ground, thanks to its miniscule speed. The pilot, Ivan Gorditch, closed his eyes and took off his helmet. After setting a course straight for the sun, he liked to let the steering column alone and catch some z's with tightly shut eyes.

"Ivan, take a look at these ballsy Romanians!" shouted the junior pilot, who'd been resting in the back. "They don't even hide anymore."

Ivan unwilling pulled his eyes open and steered the plane into the horizontal flatness. In this light, the earth looked bright green. The chain of trucks crawling toward the border with Italy looked to him like a caterpillar, and the earth – like an apple. Ivan blinked and saw a vehicle with a cistern in back amidst the column. A brazen Romanian had climbed right out of that cistern.

"More likely a Moldovan," shouted Ivan. "Looks like the Romanians have started smuggling them into Italy. That's a hoot!"

"A hoot and a half!" said the second pilot, a rookie. "Yesterday on the Internet I saw pictures of truck drivers crossing the border from Mexico to the US. I'll tell you, those Mexicans hide in all kinds of places."

"Moldovans are more resourceful," said Ivan, disagreeing. "In my opinion ..."

The colleagues argued for a bit about which migrants were harder to catch, Mexicans or Moldovans. In the end, they agreed it was Moldovans. The column meanwhile had crawled within spitting distance of the border.

The cistern must be full of Moldovans. They had to report their findings back to the ground. Or did they? In any case, they had to be vicious to the column. Illegal Moldovans were a thorn in the Croats' sides, for they too tried all means, legal and extralegal, to get to Italy.

"Let's bomb this column back to the Stone Age!" suggested Ivan.

"Ivan, have you lost it?" asked the second pilot, surprised. "We've only got two bombs, and they're just replicas."

"We'll get someone else to do it!"

"How's that?"

Ivan let loose with a horse's laugh, then logged on the NATO air patrol frequency.

"Paradox, Paradox, this is Symposium," he shouted excitedly. "Symposium speaking. Do you read me?"

"Loud and clear, Symposium." The voice with a British accent could be heard in their earphones. And it spoke English!

"We've got a huge column of armed Serbs penetrating the Italian side on our patrol," shouted Ivan. "A downright invasion, blast those bastards!"

"That right?" Doubt could be discerned in the voice of Paradox. "You sure it's not like last time, Symposium? When we smashed two Turkish buses to smithereens?"

"The buses were green, so I thought, Waddaya know, Islamic warriors …" said Ivan. He sounded hurt.

"Alright," sighed Symposium, "I'm coming over to you."

"Where are you?" asked Ivan, aka Paradox.

"Over the Atlantic," said Symposium. "Be there in two minutes. Where am I aiming?"

"Third vehicle from the head," said Paradox. "There's a big fat bearded Serb sitting on top of the truck. Sitting

The Good Life Elsewhere

there, the rat bastard, all smiles! Let him burn!"

"I got him. I got him," explained Symposium. "He's pretty satisfied with himself, the bastard. I'm sure he's remembering all those Albanians he killed in Kosovo."

"I'm sure!" repeated Ivan joyously. He was quietly laughing to himself. "I'll tell you what else, Symposium. It seems to me, he's got a familiar face. I think I've seen him, this Serb, on the list of war criminals on The Hague's Most Wanted list."

"Bingo," shouted Symposium. "We've hit the jackpot."

The road beneath the crop duster was colored by a black rose of smoke. Then another, and another, and the column of Romanian truck drivers, on their way to pick up more wine, were turned into an entire garden of black roses. Ivan and his copilot circled above, then picked up altitude and flew toward the sun. A little while later, Symposium came back on the radio to let them know his superiors were planning on giving him a medal. Symposium promised to stand his Croatian friends a glass of vodka. The Croatians, of course, agreed; the colleagues had a nice meal that evening in Zagreb.

And for their latest attempt at aggression, the Serbian government was made to pay a fine to the European Union.

48

"This is quite a legacy you left me, Mister President," whispered the Speaker of Parliament, Marian Lupu. He took a seat on Vladimir Voronin's couch. "Quite a legacy."

Briefcases in hand, the advisors exited the office of the head of the government, which Lupu had recently become. Each advisor was green with envy; their briefcases overflowed with heaps of paper. Their reports had been deplorable. Moldova had been the poorest nation in Europe for the last fifteen or so years. There was no industry, no agriculture, and the population was taking flight. Lupu cursed up a storm—in French, since he was cultured and knew five languages—and got to thinking. It wasn't that the general poverty of Moldova was distressing to him.

"And if Moldova ceases to exist, then what?" He expressed his misgivings to a certain trusted advisor. "What'll I be president of?"

The advisor sighed, walked up to the safe and opened it with the key that hung around his neck, right next to the little cross.

"Mircea Snegur, the first president of Moldova, ordered that a safe be installed here," the advisor began. "And he left a missive for his successors. He instructed me to turn over the contents of the safe to the President of Moldova whenever the time comes that things in this country can't get any worse."

"Hmmm," Lupu mumbled. "How did he know that things were going to get to where they couldn't get any worse?"

"Because that's where things were headed from the be-ginning," explained the advisor. "It's just that then, for the first few years, we had what to eat through, drink up and steal blind. So. The envelope, Your Excellency."

Lupu made a motion for his advisor to remain present and opened the envelope. On the piece of paper was a note in the rough handwriting of Snegur:

"When things in the country are in the pits, start a war with somebody."

49

Dreams die just like people. That's what Serafim Botezatu, who'd aged a lot in the past decade, found out that fall in Larga. After publishing an advertisement in the regional newspaper that read, "Translator from Norwegian seeks work," he was pleasantly surprised when Nikita Tkach showed up at his doorstep one day. Tkach was the founder of the first curling team in Larga.

"You see, next summer we'll be going to Norway to take part in a competition. I wanted you to make us welcome banners."

"Alright." Serafim nodded. "And how about Italy?"

"We were supposed to go there in the summer, but we changed our minds," said Nikita. He was embarrassed.

"They wouldn't let you in," asked Serafim, hanging his head.

"No, they let us in," Nikita explained. "We decided we didn't want to go."

"You decided *what*?" said Serafim hoarsely.

Nikita Tkach turned red. Then he explained. At first the curling team he'd knocked together as an excuse for taking his pals to Italy had only been a joke.

"Then," continued Nikita, lighting up, "we actually started to like the sport of curling. We fell in love with it. The game has its own philosophy. And we've taken that on. We realized that paradise for us is wherever there's curling. That's *our* Italy."

Serafim listened, but couldn't believe his own ears. Nikita talked and talked, and in the stove the walnut tree was burning. It was the same one Serafim used to fall asleep under. Now he'd cut it down.

In the past ten years, the curling team from Larga had achieved considerable success. Second place in the European Championships; bronze at the World Championships. Now they were training for the Olympic Games in Beijing. Sure, they were tempted during those first overseas tournaments to flee the hotel and hide, but love for curling triumphed. And now they were supposed to go to Italy for a tournament, but ...

"But what?" asked Serafim through clenched teeth.

"You see," said Nikita guiltily, "we refused, because the tournament in Norway will be better for us. The competition is stronger. So we're saying no to Italy."

Serafim wiped away a tear, trembling like a flame, from the corner of his eye.

"Maybe you don't understand. You'd be betraying not just us, but yourselves. Maybe you don't understand that by denying the dream to get to Italy, you're defiling the ashes of Old Man Tudor? Of poor Vasily, killed by a bullet? Of the shining memory of Father Paisii's runaway bride? Of the thousands and hundreds of thousands of our countrymen who died on the Holy Crusade in their quest to make it to the Holy Land, to Italy? And maybe you don't understand that you, Nikita Tkach, are denying yourself ... "

Nikita was silent. He sighed, stood up, and left. Serafim walked after him, waved his arm in the air, and crawled back under his blanket. The man was shivering. He started to cry.

50

THE NEW PRESIDENT HELD COUNSEL WITH HIS ADVISORS. Lupu was extremely nervous. He'd never planned on taking over the reins of government. What could be better than doing nothing as a simple member of parliament? And here he was, on the presidential throne, about to start a war.

Lupu crumpled Snegur's missive. "It's easy to say, 'Go to war.' On the other hand, it *does* distract people. War …"

"Yessir."

"Ok. It's decided. True, there are questions. With whom? Who's weaker than we are?"

"Nobody," said his advisor, shaking his head with absolute certainly. "Nobody at all. Which means—"

"Which means," said Lupu, picking up the thread, "we have to go to war with ourselves?"

"Absolutely," said the advisor. "We'll pick a certain region to attack, one, two, easy as pie."

"Excellent," Lupu decided. "Let's attack Transnistria!"

"No can do," sighed the advisor. "We might lose."

Lupu threw up his arms. "Then what?"

The advisor thought a minute, then drew aside a heavy velvet curtain that was usually kept closed. Lupu's mouth dropped. Before him was a giant pornographic sculpture: Zeus and Europa. Zeus, according to the sculptor's interpretation, was in the middle of his transformation into a bull. He still had the body of an athlete but the head of an aurochs, and on his forehead there was a burning star, like the Moldovan flag. The monster was ravishing a maiden with a halo of stars above her head, which, Lupu recalled, was the flag of the European Union. The virgin was no longer protesting and was in fact impassioned. What was especially spicy, the figured moved and breathed heavily.

"Pardon, sir," said the advisor, blushing. "The painful legacy of President Voronin."

He shifted the curtain and the mechanism, judging by the fact that Zeus and Europa went quiet, was switched off. The advisor pulled aside the curtain from the other wall and exposed an enormous map of Moldova.

"Take your pick!" He put his finger to the map. "Any population point that suits your fancy!"

"What do you say we attack somebody in the north," suggested Lupu. "I can't stand them. Instead of wine, they're always making moonshine."

"No problem." His advisor shrugged his shoulders. "How about – Larga?"

"What the hell is that?" said Lupu with curiosity, putting his feet up on the table. "A city?"

"A village. They're always giving us trouble. Remember that priest who gathered a few thousand ragamuffins and led them into Italy? He was from Larga. They're all a little crazy. In the local elections, one candidate for mayor even proposed that Larga become a free Italian city."

"That's it, let's attack Larga," said Lupu, scratching his nose. "What'll we blame them for?"

"Let's drag up their 'free Italian city' idea," said the advisor. "We'll accuse them of separatism."

"And then we'll rain war down on them!"

"Absolutely correct, Your Excellency" the advisor smiled.

Lupu sent his advisor off to prepare the order, and he himself glanced behind the curtain. The bull with the star on his forehead looked at the new president approvingly. The length of his manly apparatus in centimeters, divided by two, equaled Marian Lupu's favorite number:

fourteen.

Lupu decided this was a good sign. He felt at peace.

51

In October, the time came to die. Serafim, devastated after the death of his friend Vasily, the burning of Old Man Tudor and the betrayal of Nikita Tkach, had laid in bed a long time in his half-abandoned home. He thought of himself as a vampire who's foresworn evil deeds and whiles away the endless years far away from everything, even blood. He just rolled around the wool blanket, unkempt as his own head of hair, and rarely went outside for air. Serafim didn't watch television. Therefore, he knew nothing of the destruction of Eurograd, nor of the mysterious disappearance of Father Paisii. He didn't suspect that the Moldovan Ministry of Foreign Affairs had advised the Metropolitan of Moldova to canonize Father Paisii as a "fervent ally of European values and a fighter for European integration." He did not hear the surrounding churches proclaiming that Father Paisii had been taken straight to Heaven, and that there, in the Italy in the sky, he passes his days listening to the singing of the angels. There was no news in the life of Serafim. There was no nothing.

He simply lay between blankets and stared blankly at the wall painted white ten years ago. He tallied the wounds his dream had caused him. Serafim understood that, by chasing after Italy, he had lost everything: Vasily, who could have been a friend; Old Man Tudor, who could have taken the place of a father; Stella, who wanted to give her body and soul to him so badly. At the same time, Serafim understood clearly, he could never have *not* yearned for Italy because here, in his homeland, all that awaited him was poverty, darkness and despair. From time to time Serafim heard somebody enter the house and he would close his eyes, stubbornly determined not to see anybody. The visitor placed food on the table and quietly left. Serafim realized it was Stella, who loved him so. He could never forgive her for giving him that Norwegian textbook.

His season had come and gone, realized Serafim, and it was time to die. He barely touched his food. Time passed, and once, on top of the pillow he rested his head on, Serafim found a yellow leaf cuddled up beside him. Serafim thought that the yellowing of leaves was like the graying of human hair.

"And what made you grow old, and who betrayed you?" he asked the leaf. "And where are your dreams weeping now, you poor thing?"

He cradled the leaf in his hands and brought it out to the yard. Just then, there was an explosion on the outskirts of Larga. The village, which sat atop a hill on the lip of a river, was being shelled by the Moldovan Army. At first the artillerymen had to calibrate their shots and a series of shells overshot their mark. The slice of land on which Larga lay began to slowly slide into the river.

Larga entered the water like a ship, and began to float.

Serafim couldn't believe his eyes. With trembling hands he set the leaf down on the ground and looked around. The village really was floating. The sky above them skated slowly by, and the waves of the Dniester gently lapped against Larga's earth. The village, an island now, was taken even further along by the current. Serafim thought they'd float right down to the Black Sea, and then – straight on to Italy. Somewhere in the distance the impotent, spiteful soldiers were wildly waving their arms. From the other side of the village people ran up to Serafim, happily shouting something. In front of them all, running weightlessly, just like a little leaf, was Stella, and Serafim for the first time in many years thought that perhaps they had a future together. Of course, he'd need money for a wedding, but they could earn it in Italy, couldn't they? Larga floated on, rocking gently, toward the sea. Toward the ocean, cleansed by the ashes of Vasily Lungu. Through the breeze, where Father Paisii's spirit was floating with them.

Larga approached the sea.

The villagers came ever closer and Serafim went out to meet them, opening his heart and his arms. He smiled.

"Straight on till Italy, Admiral!" he heard somebody say.

COCAINE BY PITIGRILLI

Paris in the 1920s – dizzy and decadent. Where a young man can make a fortune with his wits … unless he is led into temptation. Cocaine's dandified hero Tito Arnaudi invents lurid scandals and gruesome deaths, and sells these stories to the newspapers. But his own life becomes even more outrageous when he acquires three demanding mistresses. Elegant, witty and wicked, Pitigrilli's classic novel was first published in Italian in 1921 and retains its venom even today.

SOME DAY BY SHEMI ZARHIN

On the shores of Israel's Sea of Galilee lies the city of Tiberias, a place bursting with sexuality and longing for love. The air is saturated with smells of cooking and passion. Some Day is a gripping family saga, a sensual and emotional feast that plays out over decades. This is an enchanting tale about tragic fates that disrupt families and break our hearts. Zarhin's hypnotic writing renders a painfully delicious vision of individual lives behind Israel's larger national story.

FANNY VON ARNSTEIN: DAUGHTER OF THE ENLIGHTENMENT BY HILDE SPIEL

In 1776 Fanny von Arnstein, the daughter of the Jewish master of the royal mint in Berlin, came to Vienna as an 18-year-old bride. She married a financier to the Austro-Hungarian imperial court, and hosted an ever more splendid salon which attracted luminaries of the day. Spiel's elegantly written and carefully researched biography provides a vivid portrait of a passionate woman who advocated for the rights of Jews, and illuminates a central era in European cultural and social history.

KILLING THE SECOND DOG BY MAREK HLASKO

Two down-and-out Polish con men living in Israel in the 1950s scam an American widow visiting the country. Robert, who masterminds the scheme, and Jacob, who acts it out, are tough, desperate men, exiled from their native land and adrift in the hot, nasty under-world of Tel Aviv. Robert arranges for Jacob to run into the widow who has enough trouble with her young son to keep her occupied all day. What follows is a story of romance, deception, cruelty and shame. Hlasko's writing combines brutal realism with smoky, hardboiled dia-logue, in a bleak world where violence is the norm and love is often only an act.

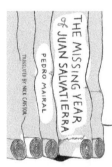

THE MISSING YEAR OF JUAN SALVATIERRA BY PEDRO MAIRAL

At the age of nine, Juan Salvatierra be-came mute following a horse riding accident. At twenty, he began secretly painting a series of canvases on which he detailed six decades of life in his village on Argentina's frontier with Uruguay. After his death, his sons return to deal with their inheritance: a shed packed with rolls over two miles long. But an essential roll is miss-ing. A search ensues that illuminates links between art and life, with past family secrets casting their shadows on the present.

To purchase these titles and for more information please visit newvesselpress.com.

New Vessel Press